THE ORCHARD BOOK OF
GOBLINS GHOULS & GHOSTS
& OTHER MAGICAL STORIES

For Eileen Carragher, who gave me "The Watchers"
M.W.

For dark, dark Kate and Colin
T.R.

ORCHARD BOOKS
338 Euston Road, London NW1 3BH
Orchard Books Australia
Hachette Children's Books
Level 17-207 Kent Street, Sydney, NSW 2000

First published in Great Britain in 2006

A CIP catalogue record for this book is available from the British Library.

ISBN 1 84121 922 3
13 digit ISBN 9781841219226

1 3 5 7 9 10 8 6 4 2

Printed in China

THE ORCHARD BOOK OF
GOBLINS GHOULS & GHOSTS
& OTHER MAGICAL STORIES

MARTIN WADDELL & TONY ROSS

ORCHARD BOOKS

CONTENTS

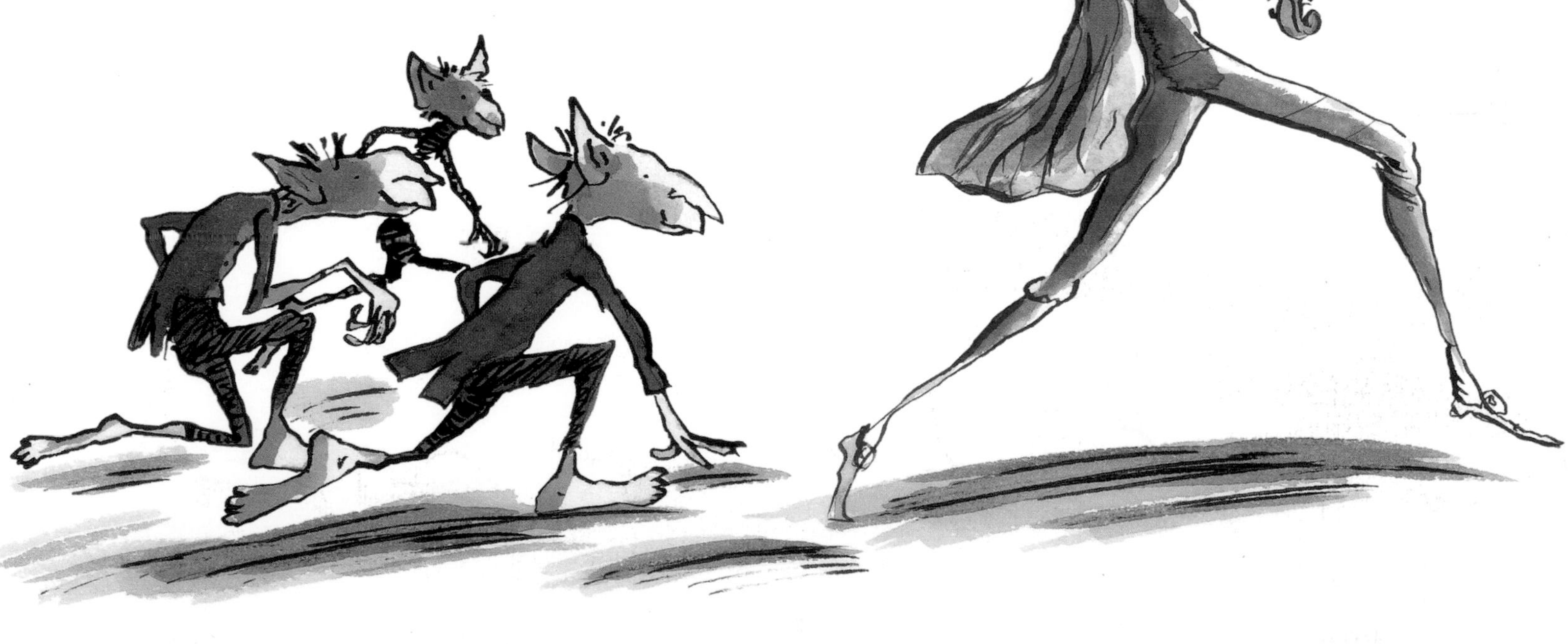

FOREWORD

I WAS TOLD MOST OF THESE STORIES AS A CHILD IN IRELAND, *living in a cottage at the foot of the Mountains of Mourne. Now it is my turn to tell them, because telling stories is what I like doing best.*

Stories grow as they pass from one storyteller to another. Each storyteller brings a different way with words to the telling, and so stories grow, and change, over time. Sometimes a new story will grow from old roots, like a fresh shoot from a tree stump. You can add bits to old stories, or work with words to bring out hidden meanings which have become lost in the process of constant retelling.

What are these stories about, and why did I choose them?

Ghouls are meant to make you shiver. That's why I enjoy the horrific joke ending in "The Ghoul of Ghoul Wood" and the slimy shapeless thing that has to be measured up for a waistcoat in "The Buggane". Bones dug up from old graves add a grisly tang to the soup that warms up "Cold Johnny".

No one can quite define what a goblin is, but mine are mean and cunning spirits.

They may steal humans away, like the cruel imps in "The Solway Bride". They can be persistent creatures, like the hairy old boggart you'll meet in "We're Flittin'". It seldom pays to make bargains with goblins, as Clever Dora finds out in "Tom Tit Tot".

My ghosts are not typical bloody-bones-and-revenge ghosts. "Dancing with Francie" derives from a tale found by Lady Wilde, and a deep sadness lurks in it. "The Watchers" is a tale from Armagh, told to me by my mother-in-law, where the gentle ending reverses the jokey mood in which it begins. With "The Ghost of Porlock" the strength lies in the heart of the tale, not the telling. It is a lovely story to tell.

The magical stories include some philosophical but practical fairies in "The Butter's Awa'", and the kindest of all fairy folk in "Tom Cockle". "Cap o' Rushes" is a well-known story, but I've changed it a lot and added lost glasses to explain the one bit that never made sense to me as a child. "The Lady of Llyn y Fan Fach" is a sad but beautiful Welsh story of a love that is lost, with a promise a lover can't keep, and "The Sparkling Field" is a warning to all who set out to steal fairy gold.

Read, shiver, wonder…enjoy.

MARTIN WADDELL

COLD JOHNNY

THERE ONCE WAS A GRAVEYARD, high on the moor. The graveyard was old and forsaken. It was bleak and bare and no one went there, for fear of Cold Johnny, the old ghoul who guarded the graves.

When the icy winds blew on the moor, the villagers heard the ghoul moaning and groaning. They barred their doors, in case he came knocking with knuckles of bone, asking to sit by the fire. Even the thought of Cold Johnny made them shiver.

That's how it was, till Little Patch came to the village. He was a thin scrawny bird of a boy. His parents were dead and he'd no kith nor kin, so he'd no one to care for his body or soul. He wandered round looking for food, but no one would feed him, till he came to Mean Morgan's farm.

"Give me hot soup and I'll help round the farm," Patch said to Mean Morgan.

"I'll do you a deal, but you must earn your hot soup," Mean Morgan said, with a gleam in his eye, for he saw an advantage – for him. The deals that he struck were one-sided, for he always cheated his way out of any bargain he made.

"Are you feared of hard work?" Mean Morgan asked Patch.

"I'm not feared of nothing," said Patch. "So long as I get my hot soup."

Mean Morgan set Patch to build a stone wall around his best field. Patch had to work hard, for the moor stones were heavy. Now and then Mean Morgan came down the lane and told him to work harder. By the time it was dusk, Patch had finished the wall. He went to the house, filled up with the thought of hot soup.

"Give me my soup," Patch said to Mean Morgan.

"What soup is that?" said Mean Morgan.

"The hot soup that was part of our deal," Patch told him.

"I'll talk to my wife," said Mean Morgan. "*Maybe* she'll make you hot soup."

Then Mean Morgan talked to his wife, and they grinned and laughed, and then Mean Morgan came back to poor Patch.

"How can my wife make you hot soup when she hasn't a hearthstone to light the fire on, to heat up the soup?" Mean Morgan said.

"I'll fetch in a stone from the field," Patch said.

"Indeed that won't do – I need all my good stones for my walls," said Mean Morgan. "But I'll make a new deal with you. Go up to the graveyard beyond and fetch me a gravestone to serve for a hearth in my house. Then you can have your hot soup. That is, if you're not feared of graves and them that is in 'em."

"I'm not feared of nothing," said Patch. "So long as I get my hot soup."

Off went Patch to the graveyard, up there on the moor.

"He won't be back," said Mean Morgan's wife. "No one ever comes back after seeing Cold Johnny."

It was dark night by the time Patch came to the graveyard, never heeding the moaning and groaning: he thought it was the wind, for he'd never heard of Cold Johnny. He'd brought a sled with him to bring home the stone. He bumped it in through the gate and started to work, lifting the stone.

But the gravestone was too heavy to lift, no matter how hard Patch tried.

And then…

Cold Johnny rose up from the ground. He made no sound, but he drifted up behind Patch and tapped him on the back with one bony finger.

"Who's that?" asked Patch, turning round when he felt the cold touch on his back.

"It's me," Cold Johnny whispered through chattering teeth. He'd no body to hold his breath in, so he had to whisper. There was no skin on Cold Johnny and no fat. He was dressed in a shroud with a hood.

"Who's me?" Patch asked.

"My name is Cold Johnny," whispered Cold Johnny, and he pulled back the hood of his shroud so Patch could see his white skull and the place where his eyes would have been, *if* he'd still had eyes.

"Mercy on me!" said Patch.

"Are you not feared of me?" whispered Cold Johnny.

"I'm not feared of nothing," said Patch.

"I'm up here to fetch a gravestone for the hearth, so the good wife can heat up my soup."

"Hot soup!" sighed Cold Johnny. "What wouldn't I do for hot soup?"

"I'll do a deal with you," Patch said quickly. "Give me a heave with this stone, and I'll bring you hot soup when the good wife has made it."

"You're on!" said Cold Johnny, and he spat on his wrist bone and shook hands with Patch.

Together they raised the gravestone, and Cold Johnny helped Patch lay it on the sled.

"Be sure you come back with my soup," Cold Johnny said, "for it's freezy up here, and my old bones are cold."

Patch dragged his sled back to Mean Morgan's farm at the edge of the village. Mean Morgan came to the door, and Patch dragged in the gravestone and laid it on the hearth.

"How come he's back?" Mean Morgan said to his wife. "What happened to Cold Johnny? No one comes back when they've seen Cold Johnny."

"Never mind how he did it," said Mean Morgan's wife. "We'll send him up there again, and this time he'll never come back, for no one in this world has been twice to Cold Johnny."

"My wife would make your hot soup for you," Mean Morgan told Patch, "but she has no wood to put on her fire, and so she can't do it."

"Hot soup was our deal," said Patch. "I'll fetch some wood for the fire from the farm."

"My wood is too green for burning," Mean Morgan said. "We'll make a new deal. Go back to the graveyard beyond with an axe, and fetch me some old coffin boards chopped in bits. Then we'll have good wood for the fire, and my wife can heat up your soup. That is, if you're not feared of coffins and them that is in 'em."

"I'm not feared of nothing," said Patch. "So long as I get my hot soup."

Patch went off up the moor to the graveyard beyond, and in through the gates to the graves, with his axe and a spade. He dug up some coffins and started to break them up for firewood, when up through the earth came Cold Johnny, with a clatter of bones and a cough.

"You're back," said Cold Johnny. "Where's my hot soup?"

"The good wife has sent me for wood for her fire, to heat up the soup," said Patch. "You help me break up the boards and load them on the sled, and I'll come back when I've got the hot soup."

"Be sure you come back with my soup," said Cold Johnny, "for it's freezy up here, and my old bones are cold."

13

GOBLINS, GHOULS & GHOSTS

Patch went back to the farm with the firewood on his sled, and Cold Johnny went back down below, with nothing to warm him but ancient tree roots that had worked their way into his home.

"Back again! And he's brought us our wood!" Mean Morgan said to his wife. "What will we do?"

"Perhaps we should make him his soup? That was your deal," said his wife.

"I *always* cheat on my deals," said Mean Morgan. "The deal was he'd work for his soup. If he does the work and I give him no soup, that makes it a good deal for me."

They muttered a bit, about just how Patch could be cheated out of his soup.

"Where's my hot soup?" Patch asked from his place by the fire he'd lit in the hearth, on top of the gravestone.

"My wife would make you your soup, but we have no meat to put in it," Mean Morgan said, with a wink at his wife.

"I'll go out and kill the old rooster," said Patch. "Then we can have rooster soup."

"I need my rooster," Mean Morgan said. "But I'll make you a deal just the same. The deal is – you go back to the graveyard and find me a bone for the soup. Then you'll have your hot soup. That is, if you're not feared of bones and them they belonged to."

"I'm not feared of nothing," said Patch. "So long as I get my hot soup."

Patch went back to the graveyard beyond and started to look round the coffin he'd chopped up, to find the old bones.

Cold Johnny heard Patch at his bone-picking, and he rose up, looking for the soup he'd been promised. He saw Patch at work, sorting the bones – the old elbows and skulls and kneecaps and such.

"Where's my hot soup?" said Cold Johnny. "And why are you tossing those bones on your sled?"

"The good wife has no meat, so I'm here to fetch down some bones for the soup," explained Patch.

"You're not having those bones," said Cold Johnny. "Those bones belong to my neighbours. You're not making soup from my friends."

"No bones means no soup," said Patch.

Cold Johnny shivered with anger.

"One bone more or less wouldn't hurt your friends much," Patch suggested, "considering they are not using their bones any more."

"I'm not having that!" said Cold Johnny. "But here's what I'll do: I'll lend you one of *my* bones for the soup."

And he took off his right leg bone and gave it to Patch.

"That's just dandy!" said Patch. "You wait here till I come with your soup."

So Patch went off with Cold Johnny's right leg bone for the soup.

Mean Morgan was mad when Patch came back to the farm, but his wife took the right leg bone and popped it in the pot with some peas and potatoes and cabbage.

"That was your deal," she said to Mean Morgan.

"I'm not having that," said Mean Morgan. "I'll cheat Patch out of his soup. You wait and see!"

Mean Morgan's wife stirred the soup in the pot on the fire. It was bubbling away, smelling good. Mean Morgan went to the cupboard and brought two soup plates and two spoons.

"One for me; one for my good wife," he told Patch.

"What about me?" said Patch. "We made a deal, and I've worked for that soup."

"A deal made with me is no deal at all. I always cheat. You ought to know that. What made you think you'd be sharing our soup?" growled Mean Morgan, and he grabbed hold of Patch by the scruff of the neck and threw him out of the house.

Patch howled and he yelled and he swore and he beat at the door, but Mean Morgan wouldn't let him back in.

Then the moon darkened, the wind roared and beat at the twisty old trees, and Cold Johnny came out of his graveyard.

Hip-hop-hip-hoppity-hop, Cold Johnny came down from the graveyard above, hopping on one leg, for his other leg was in the soup.

And...

Hip-hop-hip-hoppity-hop, Cold Johnny hopped up the lane and found Patch sitting down on the doorstep and crying.

And *hip-hop-hip-hoppity-hop*, Cold Johnny hopped up to the door.

He banged the door with his bony fist. The door broke in splinters all over the floor.

"I've come for my soup!" hissed Cold Johnny.

In through the door went Cold Johnny, and the next thing Patch saw was Mean Morgan and Mean Morgan's wife chased round the house by Cold Johnny. They raced upstairs and downstairs, with Cold Johnny hard on their heels. Then out through the window they went, and off up the lane, with Cold Johnny *hip-hop-hip-hoppity-hopping* behind them.

They never came back, for fear of Cold Johnny.

But Cold Johnny came back. He sat down at the fireside with Patch, and they had their hot soup. Then Johnny (warmed up by the soup) went back to the graveyard up there on the moor, where the old roots still twine through his bones.

Each night, around dusk, Patch comes from the farm with a bowl full of good hot soup, made of the best vegetables (but no bones), and he leaves the bowl there for Johnny to sup. Each day, at dawn, Patch comes back for the bowl, and he finds the hot soup has been supped.

But Cold Johnny is all bones and no belly.

So…where does he *put* the hot soup?

THE SOLWAY BRIDE

THERE WAS A MAN BY THE NAME OF SANDIE MACHARG, who lived close by the shore at Solway. He had the finest farm there was for ten miles and more. Sandie was not a rich man to begin with, but he worked hard and cared for his land and his cows and his sheep. He was fair and straightforward in all his dealings, and he did well in all things, but never so well as the day that he brought home his bride.

Jeanie Gaw was a beautiful girl with raven-black hair and eyes that were soft as the night. Sandie wasn't the first who had asked for her hand, but he was the first she had loved, because he was honest and kind, and a man of his word. It was Sandie she loved, not his farm nor his money.

"Will you wed me?" asked Sandie, straight out and simple.

"I will," said Jeanie.

It was done in a twinkling, with no fuss or quarrel, nor talk of bride price or dowry. There was no stupid talking like that. She knew he was her man when she clapped her eyes on him, and he knew she was his woman. It is called love at first sight.

It worked well for Sandie Macharg and Jeanie. They married and prospered, and soon they had children: two boys and a girl, one child for each year they'd been married.

All would have been well, but for the evil goblins men call sea elves, who lived by the shore near their farm.

One day the goblins saw Jeanie walking down by the waves, and her beauty bewitched them. It is a rare kind of beauty that bewitches evil folk who live by snares and enchantment, but that's how it is when a girl with raven-black hair and eyes that are soft as the night walks on the shore, holding her child in her arms. She was singing songs to ease the pain of her baby's teething, and the sweetness of her singing drew the goblins as much as her beautiful face, for it showed she had beauty within. They wanted her goodness all for themselves.

"We'll take Sandie's wife and enchant her and carry her under the waves," they decided, never minding one bit that she'd be lost to her children and Sandie, the man she loved and who loved her.

One evening, just before dusk, Sandie came down through the whins to the forlorn shore near his house. There were two old wrecks on the shore, cast up long ago. Sandie's way was to fasten his long net between the wrecks and wait there till the tide came swirling in. When the tide brought the fish, they caught in the net, and then Sandie would wade out and spear them.

Sandie waited alone for the tide, alone with the sound of the sea as it rolled the loose stones on the shore.

There was that sound…and then came another.

The *tap-tap-tap* of an axe.

The *tap-tap-tap* was coming from the wrecks, Sandie had no doubt about that. He heard an axe tapping…but how could there be an axe tapping when there was no one there but himself?

It was very strange.

Sandie was no more than a few feet from the wrecks. He could hear, clear as clear, sounds like the comings and goings of people on the old rotting boards, but there were no people to see.

Sandie's heart filled with terror.

It couldn't be…but it was.

He looked at the wrecks and saw small shafts of lantern light shining through the old planks where the wood seams had parted, as though someone was there, hard at work.

Then a thin voice piped up from one of the wrecks, the one ten feet away to his left.

"Brother, what do you do now?" asked the voice. It was a shrill voice, like no human voice, the voice of a goblin.

Another shrill voice answered from the second wreck, several feet away to his right, at the far end of the net.

"I'm making a wife for Sandie Macharg!" the second goblin gloated. "A wife carved from wood that will turn into something like flesh. We'll leave the wood-wife to deceive him this night, when we've taken his Jeanie away. From this night to the end of his life, the wood-wife will walk and talk beside Sandie Macharg as though she was his Jeanie, but she'll have no soul, and she'll break his heart with her cold ways."

"This night we steal Jeanie Macharg!" said the first voice. "This night it must be, and no other."

The two goblins giggled and laughed at the fate they had planned for Macharg and his wife.

"No other it is!" Sandie thought to himself. "If I keep Jeanie close by me through this long night, we'll be all right. If I don't let her out of the house, I can still save her life."

Sandie left his nets tied to the wrecks, for he was too scared to go near them. He moved sideways, well clear of the wrecks, before he quit the shore. Then he ran home the back way over the old rocky fields to his house. He ran like the wind, never minding the brambles that ripped at his legs.

When he got home, he bolted the green door at the front of his house and the little black door that led out the back. He ran round inside the house like a man who'd gone wild. He barred all the doors and nailed boards over the windows.

"What are you doing?" asked Jeanie. "If you nail up the windows like that, we can't use them."

"Trust me through this long night. I'm doing what has to be done," was all Sandie would say, for he was afraid he would scare Jeanie out of her wits if he told her the goblins were planning to steal her away from her home and her children.

"That's no answer at all!" Jeanie thought to herself.

"Trust me, love," Sandie repeated.

Her heart told her to trust him, though she was filled with fear of what she didn't know and he wouldn't say.

Next Sandie lifted his three children out of their beds and put them in the kitchen, all round the fire, where he could see them and know they were safe from evil. Then he stacked wood on the fire, till it blazed so hot that the burning sparks blew out up the chimney, so nothing could get in that way.

"You'll set fire to the house!" Jeanie warned.

"I'm doing what has to be done," Sandie said.

He couldn't find the right words to explain the danger she was in without scaring her out of her wits, but he kept on piling wood on the fire.

"I trust you with my life," Jeanie said.

By this time his fear had a grip on his wife and the house, for he'd brought it back from the shore with him.

He knew that the goblins would come, and they came, slipping up from the shore in the night.

The old timber frame of the roof creaked in the wind, and the rain rattled down on the thatch, and there was a muttering and moaning, not words that they knew, but strange goblin-words.

There was a whining and scuttling and scratching, as though rats were outside the walls, trying to work their way in. The children tossed and turned, and their small bodies gleamed with sweat as they slept round the fire.

"If you mind the children, I'll go out to the pump and fetch in some water to bathe them," Jeanie suggested.

"Stay where you are," Sandie ordered her. "You must not leave the house till this long night is over."

"But…"

"Trust me, Jeanie," said Sandie again, and he hugged her.

Midnight came, and they heard a horse gallop up the lane. Its rider dismounted and banged at the door with both fists.

"Mrs Macharg! Mrs Macharg! Are you there?" called the rider who'd come to their door.

"I'm here. What ails you?" Sandie's wife called. She got up to go to the door, but before she could reach it, Sandie grabbed her and pulled her back down on her chair.

"You must come this instant, Mrs Macharg," called the rider. "You're wanted at the Lauries' big house. Mrs Laurie's time has come. Her baby will be born before dawn, and the poor woman needs you to help her and her baby."

"I've got to go," Jeanie argued, and started to struggle with Sandie. "I promised Mrs Laurie I'd be her midwife, when her time came."

"You must not leave this house till this long night is over," Sandie said, tightening his grip and forcing her to stay in the chair. "Say nothing, and stop where you are."

Then screeching and wailing sounds came from the yard, animal sounds filled with fear, and a smell of burning crept into the house.

"Your big fire has set light to the house. I knew that it would!" cried Jeanie.

Sandie peered out through a gap in the boards to see what was happening. Flames and smoke billowed around the farmyard. The barn was on fire, and the haystack was smouldering. The trees and the hedges were burning. The whole farm seemed to be blazing around them, with a glowing firelight like no light that he'd ever seen.

Voices started shouting to Jeanie, calling her by her name.

"For love of your life, leave the house, Mrs Macharg!"

"Your beasts are burning alive, Mrs Macharg! The fire has your barn!"

"You'll be roasted beef, Mrs Macharg! The blackbirds will have you for dinner."

"If you come out quick, you might save yourself, Mrs Macharg."

"Never mind me, save my children!" cried Jeanie. She ran to break open the door that Sandie had barred tight shut. Sandie grabbed her and she struggled. He dragged her back from the door and held her as tight as he could.

"Trust me," he whispered to her. "Our children won't die, and neither will we. We'll get through, so long as we stay in the house."

She looked into his eyes and she knew he loved her. She had to trust Sandie, for his life was hers, and her life was his.

"I trust you," she heard herself say through her tears. She clung to Sandie and cried, because she expected to die with her children. She held tight to him on the stone floor, with their children around them.

The shrieking and sobbing and wailing and weeping went on and on and on outside, and so did the calling of her name. It seemed as if it would go on forever, but then it all came to a stop, quite suddenly, as though someone had turned off a tap.

There was a muttering out in the yard, and grumbling, and curses, as though the goblins were wondering what to do next.

The flames in the yard faded slowly away, and the muttering ceased, as though they had given up trying. Then there was a crash and a bang, as something was tossed at the door.

"That's a present for Mrs Macharg!" called a voice full of malice and spite, and there was a long chilling laugh, like no laugh that's been heard on this earth. Then all was silent, and still.

That was the end of the fright, but Sandie and Jeanie crouched by the fire through the rest of the night, cradling each other and quivering with fear. They didn't go out until dawn, when Sandie unbolted the door.

The barn was still there, not burned, bright-painted and stacked up with hay, and the beasts were all there, still alive. The fields and the trees and the hedge in the lane were as green as before, untouched by flames. The morning sun rose in the sky and shone on the poor frightened pair and their sleepy-eyed children.

On the front step lay a life-sized lump of blackened ship's oak, carved to look like Jeanie.

"If you had gone out in the night when they called, this wicked elf-*thing* the goblins had fashioned would have come alive and walked in through the door in your place," Sandie told his wife. "It would have talked and seemed to be you, and been flesh and blood, though without any soul. If you'd not trusted my word and gone out of the house, you would have been stolen away under the sea, and we'd never have seen you again."

Jeanie couldn't bring herself to touch the elf-*thing* that could have been *her*, for fear of enchantment, and the half-life that slept in it.

"What will we do with it, Sandie?" she said.

"Trust me," Sandie replied.

"Trust you to do what?" Jeanie asked.

"Trust me to ask someone who knows better than I do!" said Sandie.

They called in all the elders and neighbours and folk to give their advice. And the end of it was that they decided to build a great bonfire in the field and burn the goblins' elf-*thing* on the top.

No one would touch the elf-*thing*, so they took two pitchforks from the barn and used them to throw it on the fire, into the midst of the flames.

There was a huge crackle and hiss, and the fire roared round the *thing* and burned it, till it was no more.

It screamed as it burned, but not with the voice of any woman on earth, nor any man.

That is not quite the end of this story. In the fire ashes, they found a cup made of metal, shining bright as the flames that had burned the goblins' elf-*thing*.

"I'm not having that cup in my house!" Jeanie said when she saw it, for she knew it must be an elf-cup. It must have belonged to the goblins, and she wanted nothing they had owned in her home.

"Trust me," Sandie said. "The cup is a beautiful thing, and the flames of the fire have burned all the badness away."

They took the cup into the house, and each day they drank from the cup together, sharing their love with each other, as do all who have learned how to trust.

The strength of their love and their trust was too much for the goblins… much too much.

No evil ever came to their house again.

THE BUTTER'S AWA'

THERE ONCE WAS A WISE FARMER who knew how to work with the strange folk. They looked after his cows, and in return the wise farmer left the strange folk their share of the butter. He'd leave some good stuff in the churn, and when morning time came, it would be gone.

It went on that way, year after year. The strange folk looked after his sheep, and when shearing time came, it was done twice as fast as the farmer's men could have done it working alone. The wise farmer gave the strange folk the four best fleeces to keep, as their reward.

The strange folk helped with his harvest. The work was done four times as fast as his men could have done it without any help. The strange folk got their share of the crop, and no one begrudged it, for they had done most of the work, though no one ever saw them.

The wise farmer trusted his men, and they trusted him. They knew he was a good man to work for, and so they worked well.

So it was, till one night a cold wind blew over the farm and the men heard a sad voice call out in the fields:

"The good man's awa',
And what will we dae?"

And another voice answered:

"Who knows?"

The men went to the house and found that the wise farmer had died.

A new farmer took over the farm. The new man knew a lot about farming, but he was tightfisted with his money, and when he took a look at the wise farmer's accounts, he started to ask some sharp questions.

"What's this?" he said to his butter man, when he looked at the book for the butter.

"What's what?" said the butter man.

"What's this butter we're giving away?" said the new farmer.

"That's the wages we pay the strange folk," the butter man said. "They help out with the cows, and for that we give them some butter."

"I pay you and the men to look after my cows!" said the tightfisted man. "I'm not paying the strange folk as well. There'll be no more butter left out for the strange folk, not on my farm."

He thought that the men who worked on the farm had been stealing his butter, for he didn't believe in the strange folk.

The next time the strange folk came looking, there was no butter left in the churn.

That night, a worried voice called out in the fields:

"The butter's awa'.

What will we dae?"

And the other voice answered:

"We'll just hae to make dae,

Wi' nae butter."

When shearing time came again, the tightfisted farmer sent for the shepherd.

"What's this I see?" he said, tapping the book. "Last year we finished up four fleeces short!"

"That's the four fleeces we give to the strange folk, to thank them for their work with the sheep all the year," said the shepherd.

"I pay you and the men to look after my sheep. I'm not paying the strange folk as well!" the farmer said.

"The strange folk won't like it!" muttered the shepherd.

"This farm belongs to me, not the strange folk," the tightfisted farmer said. "It seems to me you've let the men steal my fleeces."

So the shearing was done, and no fleeces were left out for the strange folk.

That night, an angry voice called out from beside the sheep pens:

"The wool's awa' wi' the butter.

What will we dae,

Wi' nae wool and nae butter?"

And the other voice answered:

"We'll just hae to make dae,

Wi' nae wool and nae butter."

The same thing happened with the harvest. The tightfisted farmer believed the men were stealing his hay and putting the blame on the strange folk. So, although the strange folk helped with his harvest, he left them no share of the crop.

This time the voice sounded furious!

"The hay's awa' tae!

What will we dae,

Wi' nae hay and nae wool and nae butter?"

And the other voice answered:

"We'll just hae to make dae,

Wi' nae hay and nae wool and nae butter."

After that, things went from bad to worse.

It happened quite slowly, but soon the farmer could see that nothing was going right with his farm. A cow broke its leg in a ditch, and ten sheep got the worm, and the rain didn't come to bring up the crop in the field.

The men knew what had happened. They tried telling the farmer the truth about the bad luck he'd been having, but he didn't trust them, and he wouldn't listen.

Good men won't stay where they feel they're not trusted.

Soon the butter man left, down the road to the south.

The shepherd went off to work for himself.

The men who knew how to make the crop grow quit a week or so later.

That was the end for the tightfisted farmer. He couldn't work the farm all by himself, and no one would take the places of the men who had gone, however much money he promised to pay them.

The farmer went away, leaving the house to grow cold behind him, with a great padlock on the front gate.

A voice called out in the field when the farmer was well down the road:

> *"The tight man's awa'.*
>
> *And what will we dae?"*

And the other voice answered happily:

> *"We'll just hae to make dae by oursel'!"*

DANCING WITH FRANCIE

EILEEN McMAHON LIVED ON SHARK ISLAND. She was queen of the island at dancing, for she had a light body and feet that were quick. When she danced, her eyes sparkled and shone with the love of the dance that was in her. It put heart in the old ones just *watching* her dance, and she set them all tapping their feet.

It wasn't Eileen's way to be dancing alone, for that's not what dancing's about. She danced with all the young men at first, but as time went by she settled on one man alone: Francie Gorman.

Dancing leads naturally to this and to that, and before long the young couple had fallen in love.

They were as happy as young lovers can be, and soon to be married…but it all went wrong. Death came when they didn't expect it, and Death put an end to their dreams.

It happened this way.

One warm night in April, Francie Gorman set off in his boat to catch fish. He cast his net and the good fish came into it so well that he paid little heed to what was happening all around him.

As he fished, the air grew cold, and then icy, and a bitter wind blew, so he had to haul in his net and row for the shore.

The wind ripped up the sea. The waves caught his boat and tossed it about as if it was an eggshell, then turned it over. Francie went down in the waves and was drowned.

That was the end of poor Francie.

His wet corpse was washed up on the sand, with seaweed in his dark curly hair. Eileen McMahon found him. She had been searching the shores of Shark Island in the hope that he'd been saved, but he hadn't.

Her cries brought the Gormans down to the shore, and they lifted Francie's body up onto a cart that belonged to his brother. Young Eileen walked by the side of the cart as they pulled him home. She held her head low and wept for the loss of the man she had loved like no other, for he was the love of her life.

The Gormans mourned with Eileen when Francie was buried, six feet underground, his feet pointing out to the sea.

That night, Francie Gorman slept alone in his grave, and Eileen walked alone by the sea. The two didn't meet, for how could they, while Francie was dead, buried and under the ground?

The poor girl was never the same after that, for the light had gone out of her life. So it was, till the end of November, the very last day of the month. Eileen went down in the dark to the shore and sat alone by the sea that had taken her man, and she waited. She knew Francie would come, for the last night of November is the night when the dead have their dance on Shark Island.

Eileen heard soft music, the notes of a pipe and fiddle. She followed the sound till she came to where all the dead of the island were dancing, their faces as pale as the moonlight around them.

Francie Gorman was there, all by himself, with no partner. He looked much as he had looked when he was alive, but he was a ghost, a pale ghost, whose dark eyes filled with tears when he saw Eileen running to him.

"Go back, Eileen," Francie called. "You shouldn't be here."

"I came here to dance, and we're dancing," she said, and she took the poor ghost in her arms.

They danced with eyes for no one but each other. They danced on and on, clinging together, until the dance ended.

"You must go back to the living, Eileen," Francie said.

"Just one more dance, Francie," she said.

And they danced again to the soft music, with the dead dancing around them, till the music stopped once again.

"Eileen," he whispered. "Go now. You don't belong with the dead."

"I belong next to you," Eileen said.

They danced and they danced and danced. Eileen stayed in the ring of the dancing dead people, as long as the soft music played.

Eileen came home at dawn the next morning, with her long hair all damp from the dew. She walked into the house and lay down on her bed without even changing her clothes.

"She's white as a ghost!" said her mother, and she feared at once that Eileen was dying.

All the long day, the poor woman sat by her daughter's bed. The neighbours came in to the McMahons' house. They tried to help, but there was no hope. The wise woman came with her herbs, and the priest came to anoint Eileen, and all the good folk came and spoke to her, in the hope that their kind words would rouse her.

Sometimes it seemed that she listened and heard what they said, but sometimes it seemed that she was listening to something that they could not hear.

Then, as the moon rose, the sound of soft music came again from the shore and spread round the house. It was soft as a whisper. Only Eileen could hear it.

They say she gave her life for her love, but the neighbours won't hear it said that she's dead, although she's been coffined and laid in the grave, and her Mass has been said by the priest.

They say she's gone dancing with Francie instead.

She always loved dancing with Francie.

TOM COCKLE

THE QUINNS HAD THEIR OWN IRISH LUCK, and they called their luck by the name of Tom Cockle.

It was like this: the Quinns lived in a little house by a wild Irish lake. Artie and his wife, Mary, had three children: Michael and Owen and Wee Annie Quinn. No one else shared the place with the Quinns, but they weren't completely alone in the house, for a kind thing was there that they called Tom Cockle, a kind thing that looked after the Quinns.

When there was housework to be done, they just called up the chimney for him, and Tom Cockle would do it.

"Tom Cockle! The house has gone cold, and Wee Annie is sick, and we have to be out in the fields," Mary would call. When they came back, the fire would be lit, and the place would be cosy and warm, with Wee Annie tucked up by the fire and well cared for.

"Tom Cockle, dear! The thing is that the beds need making right now, and I've no time to do it! It isn't my fault so perhaps you'll excuse me." The beds would be made, with bedwarmers put in them, and the pillows plumped up and the bedcovers turned down.

"Please, Tom Cockle! We're right out of water, and no one to fetch it, for we're all worn out with our work." Four buckets full of clear water would be drawn from the well and left quietly outside the back door, with not a drop wasted or spilled, and no fuss at all made by Tom Cockle.

That's how it was with the Quinns.

They didn't talk much about it, for that isn't the way to go minding your luck. No one ever mentioned Tom Cockle's name out of the house, but after a while everyone around knew he must be there, or something like him, for how else could the Quinns get the housework done, when they were toiling all day in the fields? Nobody grudged them their luck, for with five mouths to feed and just three stony fields, the Quinns all knew how to work hard, and work hard they did.

All day, they worked side by side in their fields by the lake, Artie and Mary and Michael and Owen, and even Wee Annie helped with pulling out the thistles and docks. And the good of it was, when they quit their work and went on up the lane to the little house, they knew they would see the lamp lit, the door open wide to welcome them in and the house all filled up with the smell of Tom Cockle's stew in the pot.

"Thank Tom Cockle for us," Mary would say to Annie.

And the little girl would call up the chimney, "You're a kind sort, Tom Cockle, whoever you are!" and everyone would smile, though no answer came back down the chimney.

Well, that was fine, till the bad times came on them.

The Quinns worked as hard as they could, but one year, when the crop was in, they had no harvest worth mentioning at all, and nothing to save for the winter or trade in the town for fresh food, and no way of paying the landlord his rent. The neighbours had no better luck…some had worse. It was a bad time.

"That's it!" Artie Quinn said to his wife. "We can't earn our bread here the way things are going. We must go over the water to your mother's old home in England. The stone house she had will give us a roof over our heads. And there'll be a lake like we're used to at home."

"It's cold, that old house!" Mary Quinn said ruefully. "No one has lived there for years, not since my mother died. You've never been there or you wouldn't suggest it. It's too big for us. We're well used to our small Irish house where we live. How could we manage that big English one?"

"No landlord and no rent to pay!" Artie said firmly.

"No rent but no roof!" Mary said grimly. "And all those old chilly stone floors and stairs! How could I keep the place clean?"

"You told me the roof was good slate, not like this place."

"What there is left of it lets in the rain," said Mary. "The slates have not been fixed since my old father passed on. The old house is filled up with big empty rooms and cold draughts."

"I'll put the roof right, and with all of us in we'll cheer the house up," promised Artie. "And the crop will grow there, not like the crop that's turned black in our fields. You know I'd stay here if I could. If Ireland can't feed us, maybe England will."

"We must go if we must, I suppose," Mary sighed.

They gathered the children together and told them. Michael and Owen said nothing, for they were old enough to know that they had no choice but to go. Wee Annie said plenty.

"I'm not going," she said. "I'm not leaving our house. I'm not leaving Tom Cockle!"

And she sat by the fire and she cried.

But she had to go. She was too small to stay there all by herself, even with Tom Cockle's help.

So the Quinns sold their furniture and said their goodbyes to their neighbours, hoping they would come back someday, though they knew in their hearts that they would not.

GOBLINS, GHOULS & GHOSTS

Then the time came to go from the little house down by the lake and the small stony fields.

"Say goodbye to our good friend, Tom Cockle," Mary said to Annie.

"Tom Cockle! Tom Cockle!" Annie called up the chimney. "We have to leave you to look after the next ones that come to this house. We don't want to go, but we must, or we'll starve."

"Tell him we'll all miss him," Owen said gruffly, and Michael looked red-eyed and choky.

"We'll all miss you, Tom Cockle, dear!" Annie called, with a tear on her cheek.

"Tell him we love him for all the kindness he's shown us," Mary said to her daughter, and it wasn't only the child who was crying.

"We love you, Tom Cockle," Wee Annie called up the chimney.

Artie came and took her by the hand.

"Say goodbye to Tom Cockle, Wee Annie," he said.

"Goodbye, dear Tom Cockle!" called Annie.

And then…well, then they just went. What could they do but just go?

Not much was said after that.

Wee Annie sat on the back of the cart and she watched the house by the lake all the way till they turned over the hill and it went from their sight. Then she curled down in the cart by her mother, and lay there without speaking again till they got to the ship.

And then…well, Annie cheered up a bit. They all did. They had to, because life goes on.

"We'll make the new place go well!" Artie said to his boys, as they boarded the boat. "It has to go well, for your mother's heart's broken as it is, leaving our home by the lake."

"We'll do what we can," Owen said.

Michael said nothing. He sat and clutched his bundle of clothes and thought of the home he had left.

"The new house will be fine," Mary said to Wee Annie. "You'll have a room all to yourself.

A nice room with…with…" But she couldn't think what would make the room look nice for Wee Annie, for they'd no furniture fit to put in the big house.

"I loved it there when I was little," she said to Annie. "My mammy kept a great fire in the hearth, and the stone house was happy and warm." She didn't say that in her mammy's day there'd been servants to help clean the house and keep the fires burning.

"Will your mammy be there?" asked Wee Annie.

"My mammy's long gone," Mary said.

"But the stone house will be warm, like our house by the lake?" said Wee Annie, who was feeling the cold off the sea.

Mary said nothing at all.

She knew she couldn't say the stone house would be cosy and warm. She knew it was empty and cold and locked up, with no fire in the hearth, and no oil in the lamps, and her mother's furniture worn with age and neglect, and covered in spiders' webs and dust and old plaster come down from the walls.

The Quinns landed the very next morning. Artie hired a horse and a cart from the man at the inn, and they loaded themselves and their things upon it and set off on the long weary drive through the mountains.

And it rained, and the wind blew, just like the cold rain and wind back at home.

They huddled down in the cart to keep themselves warm.

"It's cold, England is, Daddy," Michael said.

"So is Ireland," said Artie. "Where we're going is much the same as our place at home, and better by far than the city."

"England's not our own country, Daddy," Michael said stubbornly.

"From now on it is," Artie answered back. He was homesick and heartsick himself, but he wouldn't show it, for he had his wife and his family to be strong for. He knew that they'd never go back to the land where their three fields were rotting and black.

"Is it far now, Daddy?" asked Wee Annie. She was huddled up there at the front of the cart, inside her father's horse blanket that he'd pulled around her for warmth.

"Not very far, Annie," he said, although he knew that they still had hours to travel.

The cart went on through the day and then the cold chill of evening wrapped around them, as the wheels rumbled on the road.

They creaked on through the wind and the rain coming down.

"How far now, Daddy?" asked Owen.

"Far enough," Artie said.

Miles and miles more, in the wind and the rain.

"How far now, Daddy?" asked Owen again.

"Not too far, I hope," Artie said, and he put his coat over Owen, to protect his son from the damp and the rain.

More wind and more rain, many miles more.

"Is there far to go now, Daddy?" asked Owen again, the next time he woke up.

"Not far," Artie said, and this time it was true.

Wee Annie half heard what he said, and she stuck her head out of the blanket.

"Is that it, Daddy?" she said, and she pointed.

"Is what it?" asked her father.

"That place down there, with the lamp at the window?" she said. "It must be our house!"

"It can't be, if there is a light," Artie said. "There'd be nobody at the house to greet us."

"Oh, but it is our house!" said Mary.

It was her mother's old house, but the slates on the roof were all fixed, and the wood smoke rose in the night, and an oil lamp shone at the window. A smell of fresh bread baking came down the lane from the wide-open door. The old place was all spick-and-span and cleaned up for the Quinns.

"Tom Cockle, you got here before us!" Wee Annie cried, as she bounced in the door.

Their good luck had got there before them, in time to welcome them in.

That's how it is with Tom Cockle.

He's still living there with the Quinns.

TOM TIT TOT

THERE ONCE WAS A GIRL NAMED DORA, whose parents had died. "What will happen to me, Auntie Janey?" she sobbed.

"Well, you'll come and live with me," said Auntie Janey, and she dried Dora's tears.

From that day on, Auntie Janey spoiled Dora to bits. Whatever the girl did, Auntie praised her and said that she'd got it just right. Dora believed her, for she didn't know any better.

"You're my Clever Dora," Auntie Janey would say. "One day you will marry a prince."

It was just auntie talk, but Clever Dora looked at her face in the mirror, and she thought she looked really princessy. She took to sitting on a stool at the front of the house, combing her beautiful hair or polishing her fingernails so that they shone.

"What have you been doing all day, Clever Dora?" her auntie would ask.

"Looking beautiful," Clever Dora would explain. "Just in case a prince rides by. You never know…it might happen someday."

She was sure she had princess potential, if only she could find a princessless prince.

One day, Auntie Janey put some pies in the oven to bake.

"Mind these pies for me, Dora," she said.

"Yes, Auntie," said Dora, and then she forgot.

When Auntie Janey came back, the pies were too crisp to eat.

"Never mind, Clever Dora, love," said Auntie Janey, and she put the pies on the back shelf in the kitchen. "If we leave them there, they'll soon come again." It was her way of saying that the hard crusts on the pies would soon soften, and then the pies could be eaten…but Clever Dora didn't understand that.

"If she says the pies will come again, then the pies *will* come again! They must be strange pies!" Clever Dora thought to herself. "I can eat all I like, and the pies will come back, even though they've been eaten."

Which just shows how clever she *wasn't*.

So she tried a pie…just one…to see if the crust was too hard to be eaten. She tried one, and she liked it, a lot, so she tried another. After that, Clever Dora got greedy. Soon there were no pies, only crumbs.

At dinner time, Auntie Janey wanted a pie.

"You ate them all, Clever Dora!" she said.

"So I did," replied Clever Dora. "But you said the pies would come again, and I'm sure that they will, if we wait."

Auntie Janey couldn't bring herself to scold Clever Dora, but that didn't stop her being hungry and angry inside. She took her spinning wheel to the front of the house, and she started spinning furiously, working hard to get rid of her anger. The anger came out of her mouth, soft at first, and then a bit louder.

She found herself singing:

> My Clever Dora ate five, five pies today.
>
> My Clever Dora ate five, five pies today.

She sang it again and again, in tune with the clack and the turn of her spinning.

And it happened. It was prince-riding-by day, and along came a prince.

"What's that you are singing, good woman?" asked the prince haughtily.

Auntie Janey went red. Eating five pies isn't *clever*, so she changed the words in a flash, still in tune with the clack and the turn of her spinning:

> My Clever Dora spun five skeins, five skeins today.
>
> My Clever Dora spun five skeins, five skeins today.

"Mercy me!" said the prince. "Show me this wonderful girl!"

And out through the door stepped Clever Dora, looking very princessy indeed.

It wasn't exactly love at first sight, but princes get rich by taking opportunities when they spot them. *This* prince saw his opportunity at once, and he went for it.

"Listen, good woman," the prince said thoughtfully. "You have a beautiful niece, and from all that you say she is clever and hard-working too, for I've never heard tell of a girl who could spin five skeins of wool in a day."

Auntie Janey opened her mouth once, then shut it again. It doesn't do to interrupt princes when they are talking, and she didn't want to hurt Clever Dora's chances.

"That's right, I *am* clever," said Clever Dora, who truly believed it.

"And I need a wife!" the prince said.

Then he told Clever Dora his plan. "Here's what I'll do: you'll come to my palace for a year, and you'll have rich clothes and feasts of food. You'll be treated as a princess and learn how to fit in with my friends and my folk. At the end of the year, we'll see how you can spin. All you have to do is spin five skeins a day for a month, and I'll marry you. You'll have to keep it up, of course. Spin me five skeins a day for one month in each year after we are married, and then I'll know I've made a good bargain."

"Well now…" began Auntie Janey.

"Me! A princess!" Clever Dora said, clapping her hands in delight.

"I don't think I could let you go," Auntie Janey said desperately, trying to think her way out of the mess she'd got Clever Dora into. Clever Dora couldn't spin one skein a year, let alone five skeins a day for a month every year.

"Auntie!" cried Clever Dora, and her eyes brimmed with tears.

"I'm sure I don't know what to say…" said Auntie Janey, and she didn't. How could she ruin all the girl's dreams?

"If you've fooled me, old woman, I'll cut her head off!" the prince whispered to Auntie Janey. And the next thing Auntie Janey knew, he had Clever Dora up on the back of his horse and they were galloping off down the road.

It didn't turn out too badly for Clever Dora, at least to begin with. She picked up the princess business *quite* quickly, considering that she'd never been one before.

She soon worked out that as long as she sat very still, looked royal and didn't *do* very much, she couldn't get very much wrong. The prince's servants put right the few errors that she made, for fear that they would be blamed for her mistakes.

The next thing she learned was not to talk if she could help it. She knew it must be right to agree with rich folk, so that's what she did, and everyone said she was a deep thinker.

The third thing she learned was that she had to stay pretty. So she bathed in cows' milk and she braided her hair with the jewels the prince gave her. She dressed herself in fine satin and silk, and she practised her smile-with-a-shy-dimple and curtsy.

The prince was very happy, and so, of course, was Clever Dora herself.

"Auntie was right! I am Clever Dora," she said to herself.

Then it came to the last month of the year, and the prince led Clever Dora to a room with a shiny bright new spinning wheel in the middle and a small spinning stool for her to sit on. The room had a stout door and only one tiny shuttered window to let the light in. The floor was piled high with wool to be spun.

"Now, my dear, five skeins a day for a month, and we'll wed," ordered the prince. "That was the bargain I made. Fewer than five skeins, and I'll chop off your head!" He said it as though it was meant as a joke, but she knew by the look in his eye that it wasn't.

"I'll be back in the evening to see how you've done," said the prince. And off he went, whistling, locking the stout door behind him.

"I'll have a go, anyway. I'm sure I can learn very fast," Clever Dora said to herself, and she started to spin.

Soon the first skein was a tangled mess on the floor.

"I can't do it," sighed poor Clever Dora, and she started to cry.

Knock-knock at the window.

"Who's there?" said Clever Dora, quite scared, for she thought it might be the prince with an axe to cut off her head.

"Your kind Auntie Janey sent me," said a voice. "She said I might help with the spinning!"

Clever Dora opened the shutters and in hopped a small hairy imp of a goblin, with mean eyes and sharp teeth and a long ratty tail. It hopped to the stool and sat down.

"I made a bargain with your auntie," the goblin said. "She's been breaking her heart at the thought of you losing your head. She asked all around and tried everything, and then she turned to me. I said I'd save you, at a price."

"If my auntie made it, the bargain must be all right," Clever Dora thought.

"I'll come each day and take the wool away," said the wicked goblin. "I'll be back before night with five skeins all spun, and your head will be safe on your shoulders." It chuckled and giggled at Clever Dora, rubbing its hands with delight.

"What's your price?" Clever Dora asked. Now she was almost a princess, she'd learned how to look after money.

"My price is this!" it said, looking at her with little black impish eyes all screwed up with malice and hurt. "You'll get your five skeins a day, but you have to guess what my name is. You'll have three guesses each day. At the end of the month, if you haven't guessed right, then I'll carry you off as my bride."

"I've promised to marry the prince," she said.

"Five skeins a day or you're dead!" The evil goblin laughed so hard in Clever Dora's face that its spiky ribs shook.

Dora had to agree to his price. What else could she do?

The goblin hugged itself with delight, then danced round the room and picked up the wool and was out of the window and gone.

That evening, it came back to the room, with five skeins of spun wool on its tiny humped back.

"Three guesses!" said the grinning goblin, showing Clever Dora its tiny sharp teeth. "What's my name?" it giggled, hugging itself at the fun.

"You're called William Tell," said Clever Dora. "That's what you're called."

"That I'm not," the goblin said, twirling its tail.

"You're called Terence Arthur," said Clever Dora.

"That I'm not," the wicked creature said, and it danced up and down, like a rat on hot coals.

"You're called Frederick Darling," Clever Dora said.

"That I'm not," said the goblin, hugging its thin bony chest, and skipping about with delight, causing the shutters to rattle.

Then it hopped out through the window again, with a weight of wool on its humpy back, to do some more spinning.

The prince came up to see Clever Dora, and there she sat with the five skeins of spun wool.

"Your auntie was right. You are Clever Dora," he said, and he took the five skeins and went away, without chopping off her poor head.

And so it went on.

Five skeins a day for the rest of the month, and three guesses each day as well...but Clever Dora's three guesses were always wrong.

"That I'm not! That I'm not! That I'm not!" the goblin laughed each time, and it danced with glee before it went off with more wool.

Each day it danced a bit closer to her, touching her hair and her face. It licked its thin lips, and it started stroking her clothes when it thought that she wasn't looking.

"You've not won me yet!" said Clever Dora, and she pushed it away.

"I will," said the goblin. "I will, or my name's not...*whatever it is.*"

And it laughed at its own little joke.

The last day but one came, and the goblin nipped into the room through the shutters. It threw the skeins down beside Dora.

"What's my name?" it crowed with delight, rubbing its fingers together.

"You're called Ricardo Alfredo!" she said.

"That I'm not."

"You're called Big Hans," she said.

"That I'm not."

"You're called Nothing-at-all," Clever Dora said at last, weeping.

"That I'm not!" said the goblin, and it squealed and it squeaked and it danced all around the room, skipping over the table and the spinning wheel that hadn't been used much by Clever Dora.

"Three last guesses tomorrow!" it told Clever Dora. "You'll live at my place, and you'll greet me with your beautiful face and kiss me with your sweet lips, and your white hands will feed me my supper."

Clever Dora was doomed, it seemed, but…Auntie Janey was hiding outside the palace. She followed the goblin all the way home through the wood, hoping that somehow she'd find out its name.

Branches clawed at her back, and ivy wound round her ankles to trip her and tie her. Briars tore her skin and grabbed her, trying to hold her so the wild foxes would have something squirming and screaming to nibble, and the wood rats could gnaw her cold bones when the others had finished, and the woodlice would have somewhere to live.

She came to the dark, cobwebby cave where the goblin dwelt, a cave littered with gnawed animal bones. It was seated inside, spinning at a black wheel, singing away to itself as it worked, with the fine-spun wool all around it. Auntie Janey listened carefully, very carefully, to the words of the song:

> Nimmy nimmy not
> My name is Tom Tit Tot.

Auntie Janey crept slowly away from the cave on tiptoe. Then she ran back at full pelt through the wood, never minding the briars and the branches. At last she reached the palace, and she banged at Clever Dora's window with all her might.

"Its name is Tom Tit Tot," she told Clever Dora.

"Tom Tit Tot!" Clever Dora said. "I'm saved! Oh, Auntie Janey, you've saved me!"

"That's my Clever Dora!" said Auntie Janey.

The next night, the goblin came through the window, chuckling and whistling and scratching itself, ready to claim its new bride.

"What's my name?" it asked slyly, pinching her arm.

"You're called Peter Plumscod," said Clever Dora.

"That I'm not," it said, and it flashed its teeth at her and grinned.

"You're Basil Oliphant," said Clever Dora.

"That I'm not," said the goblin, and it did a small dance and kicked up its knees. "Last go!" it said.

"You're called TOM TIT TOT!" Clever Dora said.

"That I am!" moaned the goblin.

It screamed and tore its hair out and jabbered and cursed and scuttled all over the room. Hot flames came out of its ears, and its little eyes bulged as though they would burst, all glistening with anger and tears.

And then it jumped out of the window and was gone…and that was the last Clever Dora saw of Tom Tit Tot.

Clever Dora was very pleased, as well she might be.

Auntie Janey was happy as well, but one night, when Dora and the prince had been married for ten months, she was struck by a terrible thought. "Another year's almost gone, and the prince will soon be asking for five skeins a day for a month for this year!" she thought. "Tom Tit Tot's been and gone, and he won't be doing the spinning again. How can my Clever Dora spin five skeins of wool a day for a month, when she couldn't spin one a week if you paid her? My poor darling can't do it. When he finds she isn't up to the work, the prince will cut her head off, and it will be my fault for telling him that she could do it!"

Auntie Janey went to the palace to warn Clever Dora.

Clever Dora was there, in her frills and her flounces.

"My husband the prince won't do that," Clever Dora said. "I know his ways, and I'll make him forget."

"Princes don't forget. That's why they are rich!" said her auntie.

"Well, *maybe* he will," Clever Dora said.

"Maybe…" Auntie said. "*Maybe* not."

"Maybe…he'll cut my head off!" gasped Clever Dora, and she started to cry.

"It's only a *maybe*," said Auntie, but that didn't help Dora a lot.

"Save me, Auntie!" Dora cried.

Auntie Janey thought and thought, racking her brains, and then she came up with another plan to save Clever Dora's head.

"Leave it to me," she told Clever Dora. "But first you must get me fine clothes, like the clothes that you wear, not like the old things that I work in."

"How does that keep my head on my shoulders?" asked Clever Dora.

"Here's what you do," said Auntie Janey. "Tell your husband you've been his wife for a year, and yet there's never been a smart party in your palace, with all the rich people invited. Tell him you've dressed me up, and you've taught me to be a fine lady. Tell him it is time that his friends met your auntie."

And that's what Dora did.

Well, all the fine people from the big houses came to the party that Clever Dora arranged. Auntie Janey drove up to the palace in a grand carriage and four sent by Clever Dora. She kept her arms by her sides, and her hands in her pockets. It may have looked *odd*, but that was her plan.

"This is my dear old Auntie Janey, from down in the village," Clever Dora said, introducing her to all the fine folk.

Auntie Janey was very polite. She took her hands out of her pockets and went round the room, meeting all the rich folk.

Each hand that she shook came off sticky and black, for she'd filled her pockets with the black grease that is used on a farm for cart axles.

Well, the rich folk didn't like that.

They tried wiping their hands on their lace hankies, but the axle grease wouldn't wipe off. Soon it got onto their clothes. The rich folk got all hot and bothered and cross. They grumbled about what had happened and tried picking the sticky stuff off with their elegant fingers, which just made it worse.

"What's this, my dear Clever Dora?" asked Clever Dora's prince.

Clever Dora said what her auntie had taught her to say. She'd learned it by heart so that she'd get it right when the time came.

"It's come off my dear Auntie Janey's hands," said Dora. "She was taught to spin five skeins in a day, just the way she taught me. If you spin that much, the spindle grease gets on your hands, and it gets worse and worse. It's beginning to happen to me… and it won't wash off. Soon my hands will be covered in grease like that too."

"Is that so?" gasped the prince. "In that case you're never to spin wool again! I won't have my wife's hands looking like that…I know you won't like it…but you'll just have to give up your spinning."

"Whatever you say, Princey-darling," said Clever Dora, trying hard to look sad at the thought of no spinning.

And so Clever Dora kept hold of her head and remained a princess, though she never went back to her spinning…which is just as well, as she'd never learned how to spin anyway…

But what did she care about that?

THE GHOUL OF GHOUL WOOD

WEE MANNIE WALKED ALL ALONE in Ghoul Wood at midnight.
The night was pitch-black, for there was no moon and no stars to give light.

The Ghoul of Ghoul Wood came out of the darkness and stood there in front of Wee Mannie, blocking his path.

Its eyes burned red, and *its* long greasy hair straggled down to *its* knobbly knees. *Its* toenails curled up like fish-hooks. Drips of blood dribbled from *its* purple lips as *it* grinned at Wee Mannie, baring *its* dagger-sharp teeth.

"I'm n–n–n–not scared of you!" Wee Mannie stuttered.

"Well, you should be, Wee Mannie!" *it* said.

And *it* ate him.

THE SPARKLING FIELD

THERE'S A TOWN IN CORNWALL, and above it there's a hill called the Gump, which belongs to the Spriggins.

Spriggins are small fairy folk. On the night of the full harvest moon they come out onto the hill and hold a great feast, with laughter and dancing and lots of good food. Their tables are laid with plates of silver and gold, and goblets of diamond and ruby, all very small, befitting such very small folk.

Not many people dare to go up to the Gump at the time of the full harvest moon, but some do and the Spriggins don't seem to mind very much about being watched. Some men have come home from the hill bearing gifts of jewels from the Spriggins, gifts so small that you could pile a hundred or more on a child's little finger.

Tiny or not, the gifts are precious, and there are men who will do anything to get hold of treasures like that.

There was such a man in the Cornish town. The townspeople called him the Miser because he was mean with his money, pretending he'd no cash to spare. He wore raggedy clothes and old shoes that had been mended again and again. He never handed over a penny piece to the poor or gave help to a neighbour at any cost to himself. He hadn't a wife and he hadn't a friend. He didn't mind that, for he only cared for himself.

The Miser had heard all the stories about the Spriggins, their diamonds and rubies and opals and pearls, and their gold and silver plates, and their tiny goblets that sparkled and glinted in the glow of the full harvest moon.

"The Spriggins are small folk and no match for me!" he decided. "I'll be off up the Gump the next full harvest moon, and I'll have my share of the treasures. I won't ask for gifts. I'll just grab all I can from their tables and make off with their silver and gold."

At the next harvest moon, the Miser set off up the Gump to carry out his plan.

The moon shone as he climbed the hill, and the first thing he heard was soft music. Many a man would have stood there entranced, thinking he'd been blessed, for the music was so sweet that it was a treasure in itself.

It didn't seem sweet to the Miser. The music never reached inside his soul. He thought only of the treasure he'd come for.

All he had to do was go on till the music led him to the Spriggins.

He was careful, of course, and he crept slowly up the Gump, one step at a time. He was afraid that if the Spriggins heard him or saw him, they would hide their rich treasures.

"Where are they?" he asked himself. "They must be close by, for the music is much louder than it was, but I can't see a sign of the fairies at all."

He stopped and stood still to listen.

Then his feet started to tap to the tune, and he realised that the music was coming from *under* his feet, right under the grass that he stood on.

And just then, the ground opened up before him. Out of the earth came a host of the small Spriggins folk, twinkling with light as though they were made of crystal.

A host of small gambolling Spriggins came first, and then came the band that was playing the music, and then came a whole army of Spriggins with glittering spears, guarding their king. The tip of each spear shone in the light, so that each blade of grass sparkled as though the whole field were covered in gems.

The Spriggins were all around him. The grass round him twinkled bright with their tiny lights and the jewels they wore. For the first time that night, the Miser felt fear, and he shook, though he tried hard to stop his legs shaking.

The only dark in the glistening field was the dark of the Miser's old boots. They weren't polished, because he didn't waste money on polish.

"They are too small to harm me!" the Miser consoled himself. "If they try to harm me, I'll just lift my foot up and I'll stamp all around me!"

He stood still and tried to stop shaking, till his greed mastered his fear.

"My time's coming now!" thought the Miser, and his fingers itched for the treasure.

Out of the hole in the ground came a crowd of small servants, well laden. They set out tiny tables and chairs, and they loaded the tables with the things that the Miser had come for: plates and goblets, and diamonds and silver and gold. Then came more serving folk, bringing all kinds of fine food in very small portions. The smell of the food made his mouth water.

"It's not fancy food that I'm after!" the Miser reminded himself. "I'm here for the fairy folk's treasure."

But the food smelled so good that he reached out for a small morsel.

When he reached out, his hand cast a moving shadow, and he thought that it would betray him.

"No!" he said to himself, and he stopped, frozen still, with his hand still halfway to the food.

He hoped the small folk hadn't seen him move. If they had, they did nothing to show that they knew he was there.

There was the sound of trumpets, and two tiny figures wearing crowns came out of the ground.

"Their king and their queen!" thought the Miser,

as they sat down on the thrones at the head of the very top table…a table that was groaning under the weight of the jewels upon it.

The Spriggins bowed to the royal couple and went to their places. They sat waiting until all were served and the feast could begin.

"The richest jewels will be next to the king and the queen," thought the Miser. "I'll have to move fast when I make my grab from their table. I'll scoop the lot into my hat! Then I'll be off down the Gump, before they have time to catch me with their curses."

He slipped his hat off and crept forward, with his eyes fixed on the treasures.

Now, maybe the Spriggins saw his boots move, or maybe they'd spotted his shadow when he had reached out for the food, or maybe they had known all along that he was there…whatever it was, he'd been spotted.

If he'd forgotten his greed for a moment and looked around him, he'd have seen that the small army of soldiers had moved themselves forward. They lined up on the ground round his boots. He'd have seen the thin ropes, like threads of silk, that they'd cast round him.

"Now!" thought the Miser, and he reached out to grab for the treasure.

Someone whistled.

The Spriggins all pulled at their ropes, dragging him down like a fly in a glistening web that was made of a thousand of their fine threads, as strong as steel.

The Miser struggled to escape, but the tiny creatures swarmed up his arms and onto his body, pinching and piercing his skin with their needle-sharp spears, like an army of stinging ants.

He yowled and he howled with the pain, as they nicked at his skin, but they didn't stop. They were all over him, dancing and laughing with glee. They climbed on his nose and made faces, and they nipped at his cheeks, till the blood showed in red dots on his flesh, as though he had scraped himself shaving. Then…

"Away away! I smell the day!" cried their king.

And they disappeared underground… All in a flash, they were gone.

The Miser lay out on the Gump, tangled up in the threads of the web, with the damp of the earth creeping into his clothes.

Filled with fear and despair, he tried to fight his way out of the web. He struggled and tore at the gossamer strands, till at last he managed to break free.

The Miser ran back down to the streets of the town, not stopping to pick up his hat and never once looking back, for fear of what might be coming behind him. The only jewels he had to show for his scheming were the ruby-red speckles of blood on his dirty old clothes. The only music he heard was the sound of his chattering teeth, when he climbed into bed and hid his head under the old sacking that was his bedspread.

The Spriggins were safe in their sparkling field on the hill, with their king and their queen and their music, for the old Miser never tried stealing their treasures again.

He was too scared to go back for his hat and too ashamed to tell anyone how he had lost it, or where.

Perhaps it's still there, on the Gump.

THE LADY OF LLYN Y FAN FACH

THE WIDOW GLYNN HAD ONLY ONE SON, and his name was Rhys. He herded their cattle on the Black Mountains in Wales.

One day, Rhys was far from home. He settled down by the side of a cold beautiful lake called Llyn y Fan Fach to eat the plain food that his mother had given him for his midday meal.

As Rhys was eating his bread, a shimmer of light made him look up.

He saw a lady rise from under the water and come gliding toward him, soft as a swan. A herd of milk-white cows followed her over the lake.

He knew she was no mortal woman, and he should have been scared, but she turned her head to him and smiled, and she swirled her white cloak.

"Come to me!" Rhys called to the Lady.

She stopped, but there was no ripple around the silver sandals she wore on her feet, and she cast no shadow.

"I cannot come. You are not as I am," said the Lady. "You do not see what I see."

"Come to me!" Rhys repeated. He held out the bread that his mother had made. "Share my bread, and you'll be one with me."

"Your bread is baked too hard for me!" the Lady said, laughing at Rhys, and she gathered her cloak around her. Then she was gone, and so were the white cows. They disappeared into the lake.

When Rhys reached home, the Widow was waiting for him by the gate, and she knew at once that something was wrong, for he walked like a man in a trance.

"What ails you, my son?" asked the Widow.

He told her about the beautiful lady he had seen at Llyn y Fan Fach, and her herd of white cows.

"She is not as I am, but I love her," he said. "I called her to break bread with me and she said my bread was too hard. But, Mother, I think she was just teasing me. How can I win the heart of the lake lady?"

"My poor innocent son!" laughed the Widow. "You know nothing at all of women. If she's teasing you, then her heart has been won. Just play along with the teasing!"

The next day, Rhys went back to the lake, but this time the Widow had baked his bread light, so it was more like fresh dough than baked bread.

The Lady rose out of the lake. Her white cloak swirled round her, and her silver sandals shone in the sunlight. She was calling her cows by strange names, names that Rhys had never heard cows called before.

"Come to me!" Rhys called, running down to the edge of the lake.

"How's the bread done today, Rhys Glynn?" called the Lady, as she came to him.

"Try it!" he said.

"Your bread is too soft for me, Rhys Glynn!" she said, laughing. "If you want to woo me, you'll have to do better than that!"

The Lady stood smiling at Rhys. Then her white cloak swirled around her again, and she sank down in the water, followed by all her cows.

"The Lady called me by my name," Rhys Glynn told his mother that night. "She knows who I am, though I never told her, and she smiled as she spoke…but she still wouldn't break bread with me. She said that the bread was too soft, and she left again. She's laughing at me."

"Believe me, son, I know women, and her heart is already won!" the Widow told him. "She's playing this game with the bread to entice you."

She sent Rhys back to Llyn y Fan Fach the next day with bread she had baked for him, warm from the oven and wrapped in a cloth of white linen.

The Lady rose up from the lake before Rhys, with her cloak swirling round her. This time she shared Rhys's bread, as the Widow had known that she would.

"You've shared my bread. Share my life," Rhys said.

"You are not as I am," warned the Lady. "You do not see what I see."

"I see you. You are all that I want to see!" Rhys said.

But the Lady went back to the lake.

"She will not wed me!" Rhys told the Widow that night. "She says she is not as I am. I know that, and yet I love her so much that I can't live without her."

"That is how love should be!" said the Widow. "Go there tomorrow, and ask for her hand."

The next day, Rhys went back to the lake…but this time it was different. An old man rose out of the cold waters of Llyn y Fan Fach.

"You've come for my daughter," he said. "But you are not as she is. You do not see what she sees. You have no claim to my daughter."

"My claim is this," Rhys said. "She has come to me and she has eaten my bread. Her wish is to be as I am, because she loves me, and I love no other. That is my claim to your daughter."

"We'll see if what you say is right!" said the old man.

Two beautiful ladies rose out of the lake, two ladies

with long white cloaks swirling around them, and each one looked the same as the other.

"I have two daughters," the old man told Rhys. "Two daughters who *look* exactly alike. You say that you can love no other. If that is so, choose the one you love. Then I will accept your claim."

Rhys looked. How could he choose when each one was just like the other?

The two beautiful women drifted over the water, both smiling, with their white cloaks on. They seemed exactly alike. One looked him in the eye, and then she looked down at her foot, which was peeping out from under her cloak. Rhys looked and saw the toe of her silver sandal. The other had sandals of gold, so he knew who to choose. The Lady of Llyn y Fan Fach had outwitted her father.

"This one is my bride!" Rhys said.

"I tell you this, though it grieves me," said the old man. "My daughter will try to be as you are for as long as she can, for she wishes that it should be so. But if you doubt her three times, her wish to be with you will have no power. She must leave you then and come back to us at Llyn y Fan Fach."

The air shimmered and the old man and the gold-sandalled lady were gone. The Lady of Llyn y Fan Fach came to the shore. Her silver sandals were wet as she waded, for she didn't glide any more. It was as a mortal woman she came. She took off her white cloak and hid it in the rocks by the side of the lake.

"Your father is wrong!" Rhys told her. "Now you are as I am."

"I *wish* it to be so, and perhaps it can be," smiled the Lady, and she called her white cows from the lake. They came to her call and followed her down the mountain.

And so they were wed, with the white cows for a dowry.

They settled down happily, Rhys and Olwen, his wife. It was the name they'd decided that she'd have, though no one ever knew her real name. Two babies were born to the house, two boys they called Young Rhys and Gareth. The Widow was pleased to see her son settled at last.

And yet…

…all wasn't well.

The neighbours thought Rhys's wife strange, and they gossiped a lot, though they never guessed the truth.

"She takes her two children up the mountain, all the way to the lake at Llyn y Fan Fach," they said, "and she often goes up there alone. Why would a woman do that?"

They hinted at things to the Widow and Rhys, but the Widow told them to mind their own business, and Rhys just laughed and went on his way, though he warned his wife that she'd better be careful and not give their secret away.

"You are as I am now, and I want it staying that way!" Rhys said, and he kissed her.

"Take care you don't ever doubt me!" she replied. "Remember what my father said. If you doubt me three times, I must leave you."

And Olwen kissed him back…but her eyes didn't smile.

The third baby came soon after that, another lovely fair-headed son, who they called Bryn.

All was well, so it seemed, till one day Rhys came back to the farm with a gift for his wife, a fine spinning wheel.

"Olwen's down by the river again," the Widow told Rhys. "Young Rhys is with her. She's taken him to look at the fish."

Rhys went to the cornfield, down to the river.

His wife sat with her feet in the river, the cold water flowing over them.

"Where's Young Rhys?" he asked.

"Young Rhys has gone looking for fish," said Olwen.

Rhys searched near and far, but he couldn't find his son. Then he searched again, and he found Young Rhys's clothes in a pile on a stone, by the deepest dark pool. He looked at the inky black water. Then he ran for his wife.

"He's drowned in the river!" gasped Rhys.

"Young Rhys has not drowned," she said.

"How can you say that? You don't know it!" snapped Rhys.

And something changed in her face. She changed from his wife, to the Lady of Llyn y Fan Fach…it was *almost* as though something sweet had died inside her.

"That's the first time you've ever doubted me, Rhys," she said sadly. Then she called, "Young Rhys! Come to me!"

And Young Rhys ran out from the corn, his fair hair shining in the sun.

"How did you know he was there?" Rhys asked, hugging his son. "The corn is so high that I couldn't see him."

"You are not as I am. You do not see what I see!" said his wife, and then she scooped up her son in her arms, and she started to weep as she kissed her Young Rhys.

"I promise you it will never happen again!" Rhys said desperately, and his wife seemed to accept what he said.

A few months went by, and they went to the wedding of their good neighbour, Dai Morgan. At the feast after the wedding, Olwen started to weep as she sat at the table.

"What's wrong?" Rhys whispered, when he saw everyone looking.

She turned her face away, but she kept on weeping.

"There's nothing to weep for!" Rhys burst out.

"Do you doubt me, Rhys?" she said. "That's twice you have done it!"

"I don't see—" Rhys began.

"You are not as I am. You do not see what I see for this man and his wife," she said, and she rose from the table and ran. Rhys ran after her and he caught her down by the gate.

"I will never doubt you again!" Rhys swore.

"You have one more chance," Olwen said sadly. "If you fail again, I must go back to my father."

A year later, the poor bride died giving birth to her child. Then everyone wept… everyone but Olwen Glynn. She stood smiling happily at the graveside of the dead child and his mother.

"Don't smile," Rhys said angrily.

"I have to smile, for they're very happy now where they are!" she said.

"Don't be daft, woman!" said Rhys. "They are dead!"

"The child and his mother are happy and laughing and playing together," she said, and she stopped laughing.

"How can that be, when everyone here is still weeping?" he argued.

Then he realised what he had said and his face paled.

"You doubted me. You are not as I am. You do not see what I see!" sobbed his wife.

She left Rhys there by the graveside, with the neighbours still grieving around him.

She stopped once and turned to look back at her home. Then she turned and walked on toward the lake of Llyn y Fan Fach.

No one ever saw the poor Lady again, nor the white cows that followed her call on the long lonely walk to the lake.

"I can't live without her!" Rhys said to his mother.

"You can, and you will, for the sake of the children!" the old Widow said, and she helped him to care for his three sons until they were full-grown men.

Rhys never went back to Llyn y Fan Fach, but sometimes the three fair-headed men went up the Black Mountains to the lakeside by themselves. They sat and they broke bread with each other, and their hair shone like gold in the light of the sun.

It may be that the Lady of Llyn y Fan Fach rose up from the lake and broke bread with her fair-headed sons.

It may be, but no one knows.

THE BUGGANE

TWO MEN WHO MADE WAISTCOATS lived on the Isle of Man. They didn't get on with each other, which is often the way with two tailors competing for business.

One stitched nick-nack-*neat*-nick-nack-*neat* and the other stitched tick-tack-*lost-stitch*, tick-tack-*lost-stitch*, so men called them Nick-Nack and Tick-Tack.

Tick-Tack's waistcoats were made from cheap shiny cloth, and never did fit, with stitches missed and dingy buttons that fell off the first day they were fastened, but he worked much faster than Nick-Nack ever did.

Nick-Nack worked slowly, but he worked all the hours of the day, and he turned out gorgeous waistcoats of blue or green or gold with red seams; or red, white and blue with blue trimming; or purple and sage. The buttons stayed on, for they were well stitched, double stitch.

"Why should we buy *your* shoddy stuff when Nick-Nack can make waistcoats that look much better than yours?" the men of Man said to Tick-Tack. "And when this comes to that, they fit!"

"I'll put a stop to Nick-Nack's game!" swore Tick-Tack, and he put on his coat and his hat and went off to speak to Nick-Nack.

"As one tailorman to another, I'd like to show there's no bad feeling between us," Tick-Tack told Nick-Nack. "So I'd like to invite you to a fine dinner with my friends at the inn."

"Well…that's kind of you," said Nick-Nack doubtfully. He didn't trust Tick-Tack one bit, but he couldn't resist a good dinner.

"Don't go!" warned Nick-Nack's wife when he told her. "Tick-Tack hates you, and he's playing some trick."

"I think I can handle Tick-Tack!" boasted Nick-Nack.

"Maybe you can," said his wife, but she thought, "*Maybe not*," though she didn't say that to Nick-Nack.

So the end of it was, Tick-Tack and his friends took Nick-Nack down to the inn. They all sat down to eat a fine meal, paid for by Tick-Tack, and to drink the good wine that was brought to the table.

"This man," said Tick-Tack, raising his glass to Nick-Nack after they had eaten. "This man here, called Nick-Nack, can cut like an angel and sew any cloth that there is!"

"Is that so?" said one of the men, though he winked at Tick-Tack behind Nick-Nack's back.

"Yes it is!" said Tick-Tack.

"It can't be true," said another, with a grin at Tick-Tack that Nick-Nack didn't see.

"It surely is!" said Tick-Tack.

Then he grinned again at his friends, who were all in on the plot.

"There's no customer that you can't fit! Isn't that so?" said Tick-Tack, patting Nick-Nack on the back.

"Well, yes, that *is* so," admitted Nick-Nack. "There's no customer I can't measure!"

"If that's what he says, let him prove it!" muttered someone, making sure Nick-Nack heard him. "Maybe he's only boasting, and he can't deliver! If that is so, the whole island will laugh at the name of Nick-Nack."

"Prove it how?" asked Nick-Nack, turning round to the man, feeling hurt.

"I've a customer no one can fit!" said Tick-Tack, changing the cheery tone of his voice for a tone that was bitter. "Fit *my* customer…and you'll prove it!"

"I've never failed yet," swore Nick-Nack.

"Would you bet on it?" said Tick-Tack. "You don't have to, of course." And he winked at his friends.

"Of course I'll take your bet," laughed Nick-Nack. "What's your customer's name?"

"The Buggane," said Tick-Tack.

The whole room fell still at the sound of the name. Nick-Nack turned pale and looked frightened, as well he might.

"Up on the hill," sneered Tick-Tack in a voice that had changed to cold ice. "The Buggane that haunts the old burnt-out church. Go up there, take the ghoul's measure, and make a beautiful waistcoat to fit him!"

Someone jeered from the back of the crowd. "Of course, if you're scared, and you don't mind the whole island laughing at you and your boasting—"

"The Buggane doesn't scare me!" Nick-Nack interrupted, although his knees knocked and he shook in his boots.

"Off you go then," Tick-Tack said smoothly. "Oh...and do please give my regards to *my* customer, the Buggane, and thank him for his kind commission."

Pale as death, Nick-Nack went down the street to his workshop. He fetched his needles and threads, and his scissors and cloth and his measuring tape, to make a waistcoat to fit the Buggane.

Nick-Nack dragged his feet up the hill to the church, which the dreadful ghoul had burned long ago. No one on the island quite knew what the Buggane was, or what it looked like, but everyone feared the Buggane.

By the time Nick-Nack got to the church, he was numb with fear. He went in and sat on the floor where the altar had been. He sat there with his legs crossed the way tailors do, and his measuring tape in his cold hand, though he couldn't sit still without quivering.

"Come out if you're there!" Nick-Nack called in the dark, and he closed his eyes tight, and he waited.

Nothing came but a terrible smell that almost choked him as he sat cross-legged on the floor.

"Come on, I've got work to do!" called Nick-Nack, though he kept his eyes shut, for fear of what he would see if he looked.

Something rustled like mice in a pew, though the pews had burned in the fire, so there weren't any pews and there weren't any mice.

Then…

…*Something* came slowly up the aisle, padding towards Nick-Nack…at least, maybe it padded, or maybe it oozed, or maybe it slithered – Nick-Nack wasn't sure.

Something nudged Nick-Nack's arm.

He put out his hand, and he touched old skin, wet-slimy and scaly and cold.

Nick-Nack opened his eyes and looked at the Buggane. His eyes bulged at the sight, and he screamed and took off for the door.

Nick-Nack ran right out of the church and off down the hill, with the cloth and the needles and threads left behind him, though he still had the measuring tape in his hand.

He got home and locked himself in with his wife and his baby, scared to go out of the house. He stayed in his bed with the blankets over his head and he didn't stir until the next morning.

"I've lost my bet," Nick-Nack said, and he told his wife his sad story.

"Is that so?" said his wife. "Maybe not!"

He had the craft, but *she* was the brains of the business, though she didn't say that to Nick-Nack…she didn't say that, for he knew it already.

"It will turn out all right," said his wife, and she told Nick-Nack what to do.

Tick-Tack waited two days and a half, but no one came to tell him what had happened. So Tick-Tack strolled down to Nick-Nack's place, just for a gloat, thinking that he'd won his bet.

"Is your husband in the house?" he asked Nick-Nack's wife, with a leer.

"He is," answered the good woman, with her sweetest smile, hitching her baby up on her hip.

Nick-Nack's wife had never smiled at Tick-Tack before, and the smile worried him, for he had thought he might find her in tears, with Nick-Nack's corpse laid out on the table.

It wasn't like that at all. She smiled her best smile and was saucy and pert as she led Tick-Tack to the workshop, where she winked at Nick-Nack and blew him a kiss.

Then she went off to care for her baby, leaving Tick-Tack with her man.

"I'll soon wipe that smile off her face!" thought Tick-Tack. "If he didn't go to the Buggane the whole island will know he was scared, and Nick-Nack will be in disgrace. And he *can't* have gone near the burnt church, or he wouldn't be sitting here stitching… he'd be in his grave, or bits of him would – well, chewed bits that the Buggane left over."

Nick-Nack was working on a green, red and blue waistcoat, working hard so that every stitch would be right. He was on the last stitch when Tick-Tack came in.

"Hard at work?" smirked Tick-Tack.

"I am," said Nick-Nack.

"Is that the waistcoat to fit the Buggane that you're making?" asked Tick-Tack. "I know my customer, and he doesn't like to be kept waiting."

"It might be a tight fit, for I have to admit your customer's odd shape was a problem. If you could call it a shape," said Nick-Nack. "But if it doesn't fit at first, I can fix it. That's what all good tailors do. Who knows that better than you do, my old friend?"

They'd never been friends at all, and Tick-Tack knew it, so he just stood and grinned. He knew that he had Nick-Nack beat, for no waistcoat ever made could fit a customer like the Buggane.

"You went to the church on the hill?" Tick-Tack said. "You went and measured my customer there, as you said that you would?"

"I did," Nick-Nack said.

Tick-Tack grinned. He knew Nick-Nack must be lying, for no one ever returned when they'd been to the burnt church and seen the Buggane.

"Of course, if the waistcoat you've made doesn't fit the Buggane, I win my bet, and you lose," Tick-Tack told Nick-Nack. "It had to be made to measure, and finished exactly to fit his pleasure. That was the bet that we made."

"That's right," said Nick-Nack. "That was our bet."

Then he put down his needle and thread and rubbed his hands, pleased with the work he had done on the waistcoat.

"Finished?" said Tick-Tack.

"All done!" Nick-Nack said, smiling.

Then he folded the waistcoat up and put it in a bag, and he handed the bag to Tick-Tack.

"What's this?" asked Tick-Tack, surprised.

"It's for the Buggane," Nick-Nack said, with a grin. "He's *your* customer. *You* take it up to the church and try it on the Buggane. Then you can see for yourself if it fits!"

THE GHOST OF PORLOCK

THIS IS AN ODD STORY. It's about a poor ghost that haunted round Exmoor, near Porlock, but it isn't the tale of an ordinary ghost. The Ghost of Porlock didn't *know* he was a ghost, and that's why this story is *odd*.

The ghost was a very old man, dressed in clothes that didn't look at all like the clothes people wore then in Porlock. The ghost's clothes looked like the clothes that their grandfathers had worn, or their grandfathers' grandfathers before them.

That's how he looked, but what did he do?

Well, he didn't do much.

He didn't hop about on gravestones, or lead people astray on the moor, or try washing the bloodstains away, where a young girl he had murdered had died. He wasn't that sort of ghost, and he wasn't a ghost of the night like most ghosts, for he walked night and day, without resting.

The people of Porlock believed he was a ghost, even if he didn't know it himself… and he didn't seem to. He walked around looking see-through and confused.

The people he met round Porlock muttered prayers to themselves and hid in doorways or crossed over the street when they saw him coming.

It takes a brave man to walk up to a *ghost* and say something like, "How goes the haunting?" in case the ghost says, "Very well, I suppose," and lifts off its head, and there weren't many brave men in Porlock.

Not many brave men…but there was a brave woman named Martha, who thought it her duty to help the poor ghost end his confusion, if only she could.

The ghost often came to her farm, drifting about the yard and the lane, as though he was looking for something or someone that he couldn't find. He would stand by the gate in the lane and he'd look, then he'd wander away, but he always came back, as though he thought he belonged to the place.

One day, Martha plucked up her courage and spoke to the ghost when he came.

"Can I help you, sir?" she asked gently.

"Maybe you can," said the ghost. "Who lives in this place?"

"This is my farm," Martha answered.

"It looks like…a bit like a place I once knew," said the ghost, sounding bewildered. "But what happened to our barn? There should be a barn over there."

He pointed to a rough patch of ground with a broken-down gable wall at one end.

"There's been no barn there in my time," Martha said, for she'd lived there for years with no barn.

"The trees seem the same, but where is the well, and the old lane round the back?" said the ghost. "And there's a new stone church in the town. That wasn't there when I went to market this morning. I've walked round all the roads, time and again, hunting for my home. It should be here and this place looks to me like where it should be, but it isn't."

"That must be hard for you, sir, and feel very strange," Martha said, carefully.

"Very hard," said the ghost. "I've walked such a long time that I don't know where I am any more, though I know that I want to go home.

I promised my old Sal that I wouldn't be late coming back, but the whole place seems changed, and I can't find my home or my wife."

That's when the ghost started to cry.

"Please help me if you can," sobbed the ghost.

"I don't see how I can," Martha said. "For I don't understand what has happened to you."

"Neither do I," said the ghost. "Except…there was a strange trickster I met at the market. We played cards and I won, and I won again, and he wanted me to play on and win more, but I told him I had to stop playing and go, for I'd promised my Sal that I wouldn't be late. The trickster man wasn't too pleased. He called me names and he swore at me, but I left. He must have laid some strange curse on me, for now I can't find my way home to my wife."

Martha's heart sank, for she'd heard the old tales of card games and a trickster, and she knew what the trickster must be.

"That trickster was no ordinary man, but a demon," she told the ghost. "If you'd stayed and played on till all your money was gone, he'd have tempted you into wagering your soul on the turn of a card. But you wouldn't play on. He was angry because you escaped with your soul, and in his rage he has done this to you. He's left you to wander confused, when you should have gone long ago to your rest in the grave."

"It could be so," sighed the ghost. "But what can I do? And what has become of my wife? Where's my Sal?"

"May God send your Sal, for there is no other who can do it," Martha said, softly.

As she spoke, a light appeared and moved down the lane to the gate. Out of the light came the voice of a woman.

"Come home with me now, dear," the voice said. "You and me have had our time down here on earth. We don't belong here no more."

"I'm safe home at last with my Sal," said the ghost, and he smiled a smile that smoothed all the pain of the years from his face.

He walked *into* the light in the lane, with his arms open wide, as though he was greeting the wife he had lost.

Then the light faded away.

That was the end of the Ghost of Porlock.

He is safe home at last with his Sal.

CAP O' RUSHES

THERE WAS ONCE A RICH OLD MAN with three beautiful daughters. Two of the girls were the lah-di-dah-we-love-you sort, who praised their father and pleased him, for they were all dresses and flounces and sweet talk.

It was, "Father, dear Father," and, "Oh, how we love you," from the two of them, and their father listened with delight as they read him their poems, and told him he was the sweetest father in the world, and fussed over him.

The *third* daughter was different. She never said much. She spent most of her time managing the house and the servants.

When the old man came downstairs each morning, his third daughter would come with his clean boots.

"Father, your boots," she would say.

Boots don't get brushed and polished by magic.

Then she'd go and look for his lost glasses, while the other two sat round him and praised him.

"You're so dashing and handsome without your glasses," they'd say.

"I can't see without them," he'd say.

"We'll be your eyes, Father," they'd say, "for we love you so!"

He'd sit and chat with his two sweet-spoken daughters, until the third girl brought him his glasses.

Sometimes families just turn out that way. Some do the work, and some just talk, not noticing that there is any work that has to be done.

That's how it was, till their father decided to write down his will.

"I'll divide my wealth into three parts," he thought. "One part for each daughter."

Then he thought he would test them, to see if the division was fair. He called his three daughters in, one by one.

"How much do you love me, my daughter?" he said to the first.

"I love you more than any man has been loved by a daughter before, Father, my father, dearest heart," sighed the girl.

"That's how it should be," thought the man, and he wrote her name down in his will.

"How much do you love me, my daughter?" he said to the second.

"I love you so much that I'd give my life for you, for how could I live without my own father, dear Father?" she sighed.

The man was greatly pleased. He wrote her name down in his will.

"What about you?" he said to the third. "How much do you love me?"

"I love you as good meat loves salt, Father," said the sensible girl.

102

The old man didn't like that one bit!

"If that's all the words you can find for your love, you don't love me at all!" he said. And he threw her out of the house and in his will he divided his wealth between the two daughters who seemed to love him so well.

The girl sobbed as she walked away from the father she loved and her sisters.

"He doesn't know what love is," she thought to herself. "Love is how you care for someone."

Her crying stopped soon, and she started to plan, for she was a sensible girl. She worked out just what she would do.

First she plucked some green rushes. She wove them into a rough cloak, which she put over the fine clothes she wore. She tied up her soft silky hair, and tucked it away in a cap made of rushes. She stained her hands with blackberry juice and dirtied her nails, so no one would guess that she was a fine lady.

"I'll find someone to love me as I really am, not for my words or my good clothes," she said to herself. "When my father sees that, perhaps he will understand."

Then she went to a great house that belonged to one of their neighbours, a few miles from where her father lived.

"Do you want a maid?" asked the girl. "I know how to work hard and I don't need any wages, just somewhere to lay my poor head." What she was thinking inside herself was, "I want to stay close to my father, because he needs me, although he doesn't know it."

"If you'll work for nothing, I'll have you," the housekeeper said.

She gave the girl an old dress to put on, instead of the rush cloak she had made. The girl put the ragged dress on and hid away her fine clothes.

"That rush cap goes the same way as the cloak," the housekeeper said. "I'm not having that in my kitchen. And I want your hands washed really clean."

"I need my cap," said the sensible girl. "For my hair is long, and it would get in the food I'm preparing."

"Cut your hair short like the other maids do," said the housekeeper. "If it's beautiful hair, you could sell it."

"I'm not selling my hair," the girl answered. "If I am to work for no wages, then I am keeping my hair."

All the other maids laughed at that, and they called her "Cap o' Rushes" because of the odd cap that covered her hair.

Now, the house that she'd come to had a young master who wanted a wife. He decided that he would hold parties and dances at his house, so he could meet as many lovely girls as he could. The rich old man's three daughters were invited to the first ball, but only two sisters came. No one knew where the third sister had gone, and the family said nothing. By this time, Cap o' Rushes' father was feeling ashamed and was trying to hush up the bad thing he had done.

The two sisters looked well, but not quite as well as they might have done. They had their hair tied up in gold ribbons, but the ribbons had frayed. No one had washed the ribbons, so they didn't glow as they should. The old man came with a hole in his sock. No one had polished his boots, and he could hardly see, because he had sat on his glasses and there was no one to fix them.

All the people who came lived nearby, so they all knew each other, all except one. A strange lady came, wearing a glittering mask…no one seemed to know who she was, or where she'd come from. Was it Paris, or Rome? No one guessed it could be from the scullery below, by the kitchen.

The lady in the glittering mask danced all night with the son of the house, the young master. She made his eyes shine with delight, for she had a gentle voice and a sweet laugh, but she slipped away from him before the last dance, without letting him see her face.

The other maids wakened Cap o' Rushes in the morning.

"You should have been at that there dance, Cap o' Rushes," they said, and they told her about the strange lady who had captured the heart of the young master.

"Did nobody know her?" asked Cap o' Rushes innocently.

The next evening, when the guests came to the house for the ball, the other maids asked Cap o' Rushes to come up with them. They said she could peep through the window, and see the fine folk and the young master…and maybe the strange lady would come back again.

"I'm too tired," sighed the girl. "And I've still lots of work that has to be done." She was telling the truth, but the work that she meant wasn't the scouring of pots and pans that they thought she'd be doing.

No sooner had the other maids gone out to peer through the windows than off came the raggedy clothes and the cap, and on went the beautiful clothes, and up the servants' stairs slipped the masked lady, so much the talk of the evening before.

The young master whirled her around the dance floor as though no other ladies were there, but somehow, just at the end, when he'd thought he'd ask her to marry him, she slipped away…and he still didn't know who she was!

"There's such a big fuss upstairs!" the other maids told Cap o' Rushes the next morning. "The masked lady was here, but she went and she didn't come back. She's not even told him her name, and the young master is tearing his hair out!"

"Is that so?" yawned Cap o' Rushes.

"Tonight she'll have to take off her mask," they told Cap o' Rushes. "Then he'll ask her if she'll wed, and he is so good and kind that she'll never refuse the young master."

Cap o' Rushes smiled, and said nothing.

That evening, Cap o' Rushes was still in the kitchen, peeling the next day's potatoes, when the others ran upstairs to peep at what was happening.

The young master was sitting there glum and forlorn, when the door opened wide, and in came his masked lady again. He was up like a flash, and he whirled her away in the dance, and this time he plagued her with questions.

"Have you come far, my dear?" he asked the masked lady.

"Not very far," said the lady, meaning from downstairs in the kitchen, but he didn't know that.

"Is your father here?" asked the young master.

"Somewhere about," said the fine lady, waving her hand in the air.

And her father was there, though his fine evening shirt wasn't pressed, and his coat had a tear down one seam, and still no one had mended his glasses, so he couldn't see what he was doing.

"You've not told me a lot," grumbled the young master.

"I've told you more than you know," said the fine lady.

"You won't tell me your name or show me your face," the young master said. "But I don't care who you are, rich or poor, I'll give you everything I have."

"That's just words!" said the girl.

He took a ring from his finger and gave it to her. "Take this," he said. "When I see this ring again, I will know who you are, then I'll wed you."

"Maybe so, if you mean what you say," said the masked lady, and the next thing he knew, she was gone.

The maids saw it all, and when they came back downstairs they found Cap o' Rushes still hard at work, peeling potatoes. They did not notice how few potatoes she'd peeled.

"Well, you've missed it all, Cap o' Rushes," they told her. "The young master gave her his ring. Soon they'll be wed."

"I hope he'll be happily wed," said Cap o' Rushes, and she meant what she said, no more and no less. She hoped he loved her for herself.

She thought that was so…but she didn't know it. That was what she had to find out. She had to be loved as she was, not as a rich lady in beautiful clothes. Some men find it easy to love a rich lady, though it doesn't say much for the strength of their love.

Days passed into weeks, and no one saw hide nor hair of the strange lady.

The poor young man couldn't understand what had happened, though he guessed it was some kind of test. He searched the land to find the strange lady he loved… he looked everywhere, though not in the kitchen below, for that's not where you look for a lady.

"If she loves me, she'll come and find me again," he decided at last.

But she didn't come, and at last he stopped looking and took to his bed.

"She never loved me," he said, and he wept.

Cap o' Rushes was still in the kitchen helping the cook.

"What are you making?" she asked the hard-working cook one day.

"This is thin soup for the young master," grumbled the cook. "Thin soup is all he will eat, for he's pining away, all on account of that masked lady, and I'm fed up with making thin soup."

"Leave the soup to me," said Cap o' Rushes. "No one measures a cook's skill by how she makes thin soup, for thin soup is easy to make."

"Get it wrong, and you'll answer to me!" warned the cook, but she let Cap o' Rushes get on with the soup, for when all's said and done, making thin soup isn't fit work for a busy cook.

Cap o' Rushes made the soup, and she slipped the ring the young master had given her into it, before it left the kitchen.

When the young master finished the soup, he saw the ring, and he sent at once for the cook.

"Who made this soup?" he demanded.

"Oh, Lord! It was me!" said the cook, quaking inside.

She thought she'd lose her job if he found out that she'd let a serving girl make it, and so she pretended she'd made it herself.

The young master knew she was lying, but he was wise, and good enough to be gentle.

"Don't be afraid," he said to the cook. "Just tell the truth. Who made this soup?"

"It…it was Cap o' Rushes," she quavered.

"Send Cap o' Rushes to me!" said the young master, leaping up from his bed.

Cap o' Rushes came from the kitchen in her poor dress, with her cap o' rushes still on her head, but it didn't matter one bit, for it wasn't fine clothes that he wanted to wed.

So that was all right.

They were to be married, but her family still didn't know, for she had told no one except the young master who she really was.

There was to be a great feast on the night before the wedding, and Cap o' Rushes called the cook upstairs to her room.

Up came the poor confused cook, feeling nervous again...as well she might. Everything about this betrothal and wedding seemed odd to the cook...but then she didn't know Cap o' Rushes' secret.

"Make all the food good, as I know that you will, except for one guest's," Cap o' Rushes said to the cook. "Give him meat that has never been salted."

"At this time of year!" gasped the cook. "Meat that's not been kept in salt will be smelly and bad and not fit to eat!" The poor cook turned up her nose, for she had her good name as a cook to think of.

"You won't be blamed," Cap o' Rushes explained. "The young master knows what I'm doing."

Well, everyone came to the feast, including Cap o' Rushes' father. He'd bought some new clothes because no one had looked after his laundry at home, but his daughters hadn't bothered to get him new glasses, so the old man was blind as a bat.

The funny thing was that the butler led him to a place at the top table, beside the young master and his bride-to-be.

Cap o' Rushes' two sisters were there, but they were at a table far down the room.

"Why is dear Father sitting up there?" one asked.

At that moment, the bride came in without her mask. The two sisters gasped, but before they could say a word, Cap o' Rushes whispered to them to say nothing.

The old man sat and talked to the young master, but he couldn't see the bride-to-be and she never spoke. She just sat there and smiled at the groom, as though they were sharing a joke, as the young in love do.

The food came, and what food it was!

There were soups and salads, and salmon and trout, and raised pies and roasts. There were delicious sauces and spiced vegetables.

"Eat up!" said the young master, and he handed the old man his own special plate.

The rich man peered down at his plate, for he couldn't see what he was getting, but he could smell it, and what he could smell was not good.

The first bite he ate made him choke.

The second was worse. He spat the meat out in his napkin, hoping that no one was looking.

"What is this?" he whispered to the serving girl waiting behind him.

"It was good meat that's not been salted, sir," she said, holding her nose.

It seemed that the young master hadn't heard him complain, for he piled meat on the rich man's plate, one smelly cut after another. The old man tried eating again, for the sake of politeness, but he couldn't swallow.

Then he stopped and he started to weep.

"What's wrong, sir?" asked the young master. "Isn't our food to your taste?"

"Oh, I had a daughter," sobbed the old man. "I asked her how much she loved me. And she said she loved me as good meat loves salt. I loved her as much as the others, but I thought she was laughing at me, and that she didn't love me at all. Now I can see what she meant, for fresh meat needs salt for keeping. I chased her away. Now my old heart is breaking inside me, for I've lost the daughter who loved me the best of them all."

Then the bride stood up.

"I'm here, Father," she said gently, and she hugged the old man.

"Is it you? Can it be?" gasped her father.

And she kissed him and said, "It really is time that I got you new glasses!"

WE'RE FLITTIN'

HORACE AND HIS WIFE, HETTY, lived on a farm. They got on as well as most old folks do, till a hairy old boggart came into their lives.

Their troubles began with some words written high up on the wall of the barn, though no one knew how they got there, where they couldn't be reached without someone taking the trouble of using a ladder.

"GEORGIE'S COME" appeared, written up on the wall of the barn in great squiggly strokes of red paint.

"Who is this *Georgie?*" Horace asked, as he looked at the mess.

"Must be some neighbour's bad son," Hetty fretted.

"No one called Georgie lives here or around!" Horace said. "I never heard tell of no Georgie!"

Hetty climbed up a ladder and scrubbed hard to get the words off.

The boggart watched the old woman at her scrubbing and scraping. *It* watched, and *it* curled up and giggled and laughed, clapping *its* hands with delight. *It* couldn't be heard or seen, unless *it* wanted to be, and *it* didn't want to be heard or seen.

Next morning, the words were back again, up on the wall, but this time they were painted in letters that covered the whole of one side of the barn.

That was bad enough, but as the days passed, things got much worse, and worse than the days were the nights.

All night every night for a week, *it* set windows to opening and shutting, and let cold in through the house, so the old couple shivered.

They wrapped up in bed to keep warm, with their coats and hats on, but they didn't get sleeping. *It* wouldn't let them get sleeping.

It danced on the roof over their bedroom, crash-banging, and kept them awake until dawn.

Things got worse and worse on the farm.

It broke all the eggs the hens laid, and *it* filled all the eggshells with dirt, and then *it* stuck the eggshells back together. After that, no one would buy eggs from the farm, because of the muck that was in them.

It rode the pigs round the fields at midnight, which soon took the fat off them, and meant that they couldn't be taken to market.

It half-drowned the ducks when *it* stirred up a storm in their pond, and that was the end of duck eggs on the farm.

That was bad enough, but the last trick *it* played was the worst of them all.

Just after midnight one night, *it* barked like a dog in the lane, and Horace went out to see what was what, for he thought there might be some vicious stray chasing his sheep.

Halfway down the lane, Horace's lantern blew out, as though something had puffed at the flame, although there was nothing there he could see that could puff.

Horace stood in the black of the night, and he thought he heard something chortle behind him. The sound made him shiver with fear.

The next moment *it* sprang onto his back.

The boggart's long arms wound round Horace's neck so he almost choked, and *its* hairy legs twined round his middle. He could feel and hear *it*, but he couldn't see *it*, which made things even more scary.

"GEE UP!" the boggart shouted, and *it* trotted Horace round the yard, like a pony for sale. Then *it* whopped him with an ash stick and made him jump the fence into the field.

The boggart galloped Horace over the field to the ditch, where *it* hopped off his back and dumped him deep in nettles and mud.

Horace was left wet, cold, stung and bruised in the ditch, and all he could hear was *it* laughing and giggling around him, as he trudged and squelched all alone over the field to his home.

"I'm scared of what *it* will do next!" Horace told Hetty, when he got her up out of bed. "I'm afraid *it* might hurt you or me. I think we must go somewhere else."

"I've had my fill of this place," Hetty agreed. "We'll sell all the stock and move on."

"We sell the stock after we've left the farm," Horace told her. "We must flit first, so the boggart won't know that we've gone, till we've gone! We mustn't tell anyone that we're flittin', in case *it* finds out that we're going and decides to come with us."

"We're flittin', but no one's to know?" Hetty said.

"That's right!" agreed Horace, nodding his head. "We're flittin', but no one's to know."

The plan was that they'd load all their things onto the cart secretly: their carpets and tables and chairs. Then they'd slip away, quiet as two old mice. They'd sell all the animals after they'd got well away from the farm and arrange for the buyer to come and collect them. *It* wouldn't know they were gone until they had gone. That way they'd be sure Georgie couldn't go with them, and they'd start a new life, with no boggart to harm them.

The next night, nothing much stirred on the farm, and they didn't let on with a word or deed that they'd soon be gone, for fear they might be overheard by the boggart.

They got up just before dawn, when they hoped that Georgie would be fast asleep.

They tiptoed around the house, gathering up all their things. They'd planned everything carefully, so they'd know what to put where and where to put what, as they loaded the cart in the dark yard.

The cart was soon full of their tables and chairs and their beds and their stools and their tools, and their hats and their clothes and their blankets, and the pots and pans from the kitchen and the picture of Hetty's dear mother, Ann, and the clock from the wall of the hall, though they carefully stopped the clock's tick, so it wouldn't be heard by the boggart.

"Off we go, girl!" Horace said, and off they went, just as the sun rose at the end of their lane.

Where the lane met the road, there was an old apple tree, and the cart had to pass it.

Just as the cart passed, a deep voice echoed out of the leaves of the old apple tree.

"Are you flittin', our Georgie?" it asked.

And the boggart's voice answered back from under the things they'd piled high on the cart.

"Aye, Jack, we're flittin'," *it* said. "We're flittin'…*but no one's to know!*"

THE WATCHERS

THERE'S A BEAUTIFUL PLACE IN COUNTY ARMAGH, where an old graveyard looks over a lake of blue water. The graveyard is locked and closed now and all overgrown, but some sweet feeling still hangs around it.

One time, long ago, there were only two graves left to fill before the old graveyard would close, and stay closed, and after a while be forgotten about.

There were two families who lived in the village, the poor Breens and rich Flynns, who both knew that Death was due for a visit, though they didn't know just when he'd come, or just whose house he would visit first.

The Breens had a talk, as Johnjo lay dying.

"If old Mary Flynn pegs out first, our Johnjo's in trouble. For the last soul that goes in the grave has to watch at the gate, till another one comes. If old Mary dies first, then our Johnjo will be the last corpse to go in, and he'll have to watch there forever, all by himself there, alone."

That didn't suit the poor Breens.

The same sort of talk went on down the lane at the rich Flynns', beside Mary's bed.

"We're not having our Mary stuck minding the graveyard gate forever," they muttered.

Both families soon had their plans made. Two stout coffins were made by two undertakers, two hearses were booked, and so were two sets of gravediggers, so all would be ready when needed. That way, each family planned that their loved one would be buried quickly, and not be the last one in the graveyard.

Death played a trick on both families.

It came for the two together, same day and same hour and same minute. Perhaps Death wasn't going to choose between two who maybe were more than just friends, or perhaps it just happened by chance.

After Death came, both families knew that they had to move fast.

They raced for the priest, with cash in their hands, to fix it so their funeral Mass would be held first. The Flynns fancied their chances because they were rich, but the poor Breens had gone round the neighbours collecting.

Both families had much the same sum to give.

Father O'Friel wasn't impressed when they told him their story. He didn't like it one bit.

First he took all their cash and put it in the Poor Box, where it would be doing some good.

Then he scolded the Breens and the Flynns, for he didn't hold with their pagan talk of souls watching the graveyard gate. He said that was no word to be telling a priest.

"One Mass for the two of them, that's what you'll get," grumbled Father O'Friel. "And I'll do it for love of them both, not for money."

Well, he was a good man and stuck to his word.

Both coffins were there at the Mass, and the priest blessed both Johnjo and Mary and prayed for their souls.

That was the signal to start.

In rushed the two undertakers.

The Breens had their man on a bonus, though they didn't tell that to the Flynns. The Flynns' man was on double-anything-the-Breens-can-pay terms, though they didn't tell that to the Breens.

The two teams upped with their coffins, and ran down the aisle, with their burdens held high, bumping for who would be first through the door. Then they were out down the path, neck and neck, though maybe Johnjo Breen won the race to the hearse by a short head.

If Johnjo led the way, his lead didn't last, for the hearse wouldn't start, which shows how it is when you go to a cheap undertaker.

Off went Mary Flynn, in the lead by a furlong or more on the way round the town past the Flynns' house to the graveyard.

The Breens were mad as two, as well they might be.

"Stop!" said their man. "I'll earn my pay. I'll see you're not beat by the Flynns, for all they have money. We'll skip out the ride round the town past your house. We'll carry the coffin straight over the fields! That way we'll be first at the graveyard."

In a minute or less, they had the coffin out of the hearse and set off over the fields. They just dropped it once, going over the ditch, and Johnjo might have got a bit wet, or maybe it was just the coffin.

Down the lane to the graveyard gate came Mary Flynn in her hearse, but as the hearse pulled to a stop, there were the Breens, who had come the short way through the fields, heaving their Johnjo's box over the break in the wall at the back.

The Flynns whirled Mary's box out of the hearse, and they raced up the graveyard, while the Breens ran all the way down from the break in the wall at the back.

The Breens' men did it fast, and were already counting their bonus, but the Flynns put on a spurt just by the bend, and they thought they had it by a short head or a coffin handle.

"Our Johnjo is first!" yelled the Breens, as they chucked his box into the grave without ropes, for lowering coffins properly takes time.

There was a big *Clunk!* as Johnjo's box hit the earth, but it sounded *Clunk-clunk!* for his box tumbled into the grave at the very same second as Mary's.

Then up came Father O'Friel, the good priest, in a fury.

"I declare a dead heat!" he told the Breens and Flynns, but the way that he said it, they knew he didn't think it was funny.

"Then our families are both cursed forever!" cried the Breens and the Flynns.

"If you believe that, then you are," muttered Father O'Friel, and he blessed the two dead souls together.

"Maybe it counts who has the earth cover them first?" someone suggested.

"Fill the graves in together!" Father O'Friel told the gravediggers.

And he stayed to watch while they did it, so no one could cheat.

When the last sod went in, the two families were really upset.

"You're pagans!" said Father O'Friel. "But I'll fix you when you come to confession."

That was that.

A dead heat.

But in the black of night, long after the Breens and the Flynns had gone grumbling to their homes, up from their graves came the good souls of Johnjo Breen and Mary Flynn.

They touched and held hands as they came down the path, and they sat down together, on a gravestone just by the gate.

"D'you recall when we were young and I asked you to marry me, a long time ago?" Johnjo asked Mary Flynn.

"'Deed I do," Mary Flynn said, with a blush. "But you hadn't a field or a heifer, so how could my da let us marry? You were just a hired man to my family."

"You wed no one else," Johnjo said.

"How could I?" said Mary.

Johnjo thought for a bit.

"We've no need for a field or a heifer, the way we are now," Johnjo said, moving up closer to Mary.

"Neither we have," whispered Mary.

And they're still there to this day, watching over the old graveyard that lies beside the blue lake.

They're passing the time very well, and their love will last them forever.